PRAI~~SE~~  ~~NO~~VEL

Scottish Borders

3 4144 0097 3934 9

D0121150

'If ever Ir~~vine Welsh~~ (~~Trai~~...) ~~met Eliza~~b~~et~~h Gilbert
(*Eat, Pr~~ay~~, Love*) had a lo~~ve child, this~~ n
woul~~d b~~e the result...Hil~~arious and witty.~~'
Dail~~y Telegraph~~

'~~Exc~~ellent...A voice that is blue-collar, pro~~fane~~,
naïve and funny.' *Saturday Age*

'Filthy, smart and unconventional.'
Claire Bidwell Smith

'F~~r~~equently very funny...A quick and engaging
read, with an oddly tender streak.'
Australian Book Review

'Hilarious and confronting.' Nick Earls

'Terrific.' Susan Johnson, *Australian*

'A joy to read.' Adam Levin

'The business: brutal, funny and surprisingly uplifting.'
James Bradley

'~~O~~ften poignant...a cracking first novel.' *mX*

'I~~n~~volving...Likeable, even loveable.' *Big Issue*

'~~N~~ot for the faint-hearted, but unmissable.'
Courier Mail

'Destined for immediate cult status.'
Sunday Territorian

Chris Flynn is the author of *A Tiger in Eden* (2012), which was shortlisted for the Commonwealth Book Prize. He edited 'Terra Australis: Four Stories from Aboriginal Australian Writers' in *McSweeney's 41*, and his writing has appeared in *Griffith Review*, *Meanjin*, *Paris Review Daily*, *Monster Children*, *Smith Journal*, *Age*, *Australian*, *Big Issue* and many other publications.

THE GLASS KINGDOM

CHRIS FLYNN

TEXT PUBLISHING MELBOURNE AUSTRALIA

textpublishing.com.au

The Text Publishing Company
Swann House
22 William Street
Melbourne Victoria 3000
Australia

Copyright © Chris Flynn 2014

The moral right of Chris Flynn to be identified as the author of this work has been asserted.

All rights reserved. Without limiting the rights under copyright above, no part of this publication shall be reproduced, stored in or introduced into a retrieval system, or transmitted in any form or by any means (electronic, mechanical, photocopying, recording or otherwise), without the prior permission of both the copyright owner and the publisher of this book.

First published in 2014 by The Text Publishing Company

Cover art and design by WH Chong
Page design by Text
Typeset by J & M Typesetting

Printed and bound in Australia by Griffin Press, an Accredited ISO AS/NZS 14001:2004 Environmental Management System printer

National Library of Australia Cataloguing-in-Publication entry:
Author: Flynn, Chris, author.
Title: The glass kingdom / by Chris Flynn.
ISBN: 9781922147882 (paperback)
ISBN: 9781922148889 (ebook)
Subjects: Carnivals—Fiction.
Dewey Number: A823.4

This book is printed on paper certified against the Forest Stewardship Council® Standards. Griffin Press holds FSC chain-of-custody certification SGS-COC-005088. FSC promotes environmentally responsible, socially beneficial and economically viable management of the world's forests.

This project has been assisted by Arts Victoria.

SCOTTISH BORDERS LIBRARY SERVICES	
009739349	
Bertrams	02/09/2015
	£10.99

CORPORAL BENJAMIN WALLACE

SCOTTISH BORDERS COUNCIL
LIBRARY &
INFORMATION SERVICES

1

It's not like it's impossible to win a prize. It's just hard. There's a certain technique to beating the game. All you have to do is land three balls in the same circle. The first one's a bit of a shit, true dat, as Mikey would say. Nine times out of ten the throw bounces back out. That's because there's half a tennis ball glued to the rear of the board. But if you float it in there real slow and soft, it'll rattle around some and stay put. Then you have to avoid hitting it with your second and third throws. Most people figure it out after a dozen balls or so. By then they've spent ten bucks and if they win a plush wallaby, well, I don't give a shit. Money in the bank for me.

About ten per cent of the time the mark can't work out what he's doing wrong. He (it's always a him, and they always look the same) keeps throwing exactly the same way, not altering his action even though he's not winning. To avoid trouble I usually throw my leg over the counter and step outside to demonstrate. Most times I can tell they're intimidated that I'm suddenly right there beside them. It's all very well when the freaks are on one side of the counter and you're on the other, but not when I'm grabbing you firmly by the wrist and showing you what you're doing wrong.

The burns on my throat prickle every time. I can feel their eyes crawling over me. I know what they're thinking. I know what they'll whisper to each other as they walk down sideshow alley after. *Holy fuck, did ya see that guy's neck?*

I probably should've stepped in earlier but watching Mikey deal with this guy was a lesson in how to irritate someone.

'Yo, it's all in the wrist, dawg.' Mikey sniffed and winked at the mark's girlfriend, who snorted. 'Come on, come on, just stick 'em in there, it's easy, just roll those balls in there real smooth like y'all is teabaggin' your little lady here.'

The guy watched with mounting fury as Mikey performed a grinding motion with his hips, eyes closed, biting his lower lip.

'Do you fucken *mind*?'

'What? Oh sorry, bro, my bad.' Mikey leaned against the counter, resuming his bored stance. 'Go ahead, white bread, let's get this over with.'

I knew the mark was about to snap. I'd seen it happen a

hundred times before. He lined up his shot carefully, concentrating to make sure it went in. He knew what he had to do.

As his arm went back Mikey muttered something I didn't quite catch, but I'm pretty sure I heard the word 'pussy'.

The guy threw the ball at Mikey instead. It whacked him hard on the cheek. That's gonna leave a mark, I thought. Mikey was shouting, 'What the fuck, man?' when the guy grabbed a handful of his Dockers shirt and dragged him over the counter.

I let him get a few digs in before I stood up from my chair at the back of the stall and unlocked the door. When I stepped outside the guy had Mikey down on the ground and was trying to kick him. Mikey was flailing around madly and scrabbling at the guy's shins, not a bad technique if you're down. Best thing to do, if you can, is to lock your assailant's leg in the crook of your arm and roll over. He'll fall hard and you can drive an elbow into his chest or face if you keep rolling. Then you're up and he's down.

Mikey didn't have enough sense for that, or enough weight. He's such a skinny little fucker, all veins and bones, Freo shirt about five sizes too big for him.

The mark's girlfriend clocked me first. She went a little pale at the sight of me, her eyes flitting, just like everyone's do the first time, to the spider web of scar tissue snaking up over my throat and chin.

'Uh, Darren...' she said, before stepping back out of the way. This was obviously not the first time little Dazza had lost his temper.

'What?' he said, then looked around and saw me. 'Oh.'

His hands went up immediately in the universal gesture of surrender. Smarter than he looked, our Darren. Mikey used the break in hostilities to wrap himself around the guy's legs.

'I've got him, Ben, I've got him. Lay into him, mate!'

I could have king hit the bastard but what would be the point? We'd end up calling an ambulance and then the cops would come round, and the Kingdom would have to move on in the morning and everyone else on the show would be on my back for making their lives more difficult. Besides, I didn't want anyone sniffing around Target Ball, so I just poked the cunt hard in the forehead four times with my index finger.

'No…hitting…the staff…Darren.'

He nodded, mumbling an apology. I stretched an arm across the counter, took a plush wallaby down from the prize shelf and handed it to his girl. She accepted it with an arched eyebrow.

'You can let go now, Mikey.'

As he scrabbled to his feet, I flashed a grin at the departing couple. 'Thanks for playing, folks.'

'Yeah,' Mikey called after them as they were swallowed by the evening crowd, 'and if I see you here again it'll be *blam blam*, fucken glockjaw for you, a'ight?'

'I have no idea what you're saying half the time, Mikey.'

'That's 'cos I'm straight up gangsta, yo. Nice double team on that hick, man. He stepped the fuck off when he saw you coming at him and no mistake.'

'Get back in the stall.'

He brushed himself down and vaulted the counter, pumped from the altercation. It wasn't great for business but I needed him there to deal with the customers out front while I tended to my own clientele. Anyways, a kid like Mikey gets used to being roughed up by those he's pissed off.

I locked the door to the stall and flopped back into my chair.

'Hey, I've been working on some flow if you wanna hear it.'

'Not really.'

'A'ight—this one's a real slow beat, like *whom whom whom*, then the drums come in like this: *tch tch tch-tch-tch tch*. You getting it?'

He swayed back and forth, making geometric shapes in the air with his hands, rocking to a beat only he could hear.

Mekong Delta from upriver now is on the mic
Gonna tell you a story, may not be what you like
I'm a Westside emcee, don't know shit about rap
Won't blow your mind with rhymes but I'll do ya
*   kneecaps*

All I want s'nuff cheese to pay my rent
Don't wanna get rich or die tryin' like Fitty Cent
That lifestyle's gotta give a man a nervous tic
Being known as the Miley Cyrus of rap music

He finished with a flourish, fingers splayed across his chest in some sort of ridiculous gang sign.

'Honestly, I dunno what to say. You calling yourself Mekong Delta now? I thought your rap name was Q-Ball or something.'

'Yeah, that wasn't working for me so I changed it. My cuz married a Vietnamese guy last year and he's cool so I thought, you know, Mikey Dempster, Mekong Delta, the MD thing, that'd be slick as.'

'You trying to start a beef with Fifty Cent? He's not going to like being compared to Miley Cyrus.'

'I reckon it's good publicity, you know? Maybe he'll diss me in one of his tracks and we'll be even. We'll make up at the Grammys or whatever.'

'Didn't that guy get shot nine times? I don't think you want to be messing with him.'

'S'all good, bro.'

That was Mikey's answer to pretty much everything. It's all good. He had no idea. None of the young guys do in these small towns. I see them everywhere the Kingdom goes, baggy jeans slung low, footy or basketball shirts, caps too big for their pointy little heads. They strut sideshow alley like they're dying for a minor confrontation, for some chance to prove themselves as *badass motherfuckers*, their jargon lifted straight out of bad commercial American rap.

What sort of life is that to aspire to? Having to carry a weapon to defend yourself is no joke. I did it for long enough. Sometimes I reach for it still and then remember I'm just in fucken Wagga Wagga surrounded by young dickheads like Mikey parading around pretending to be gangsters.

It's all good. Nah, it's not, mate. It's not all good. You'll find that out soon enough.

To be fair, Mikey wasn't as bad as some, and a damn sight better than most of the shit-kicker losers that hung around the show in those country towns. He at least got off his arse and hit the road looking for work and a little adventure.

He certainly had no shortage of energy. It tired most people out but I didn't mind his constant patter. It pulled in the punters and that was good for me. If I didn't know better I'd have said he was a tweaker but I hadn't seen any of the telltale signs. The crew tolerated him, the way they did with most of the temp hires. No one went out of their way to befriend him. You had to be on the show a couple of seasons before anyone made that kind of effort.

Our ragtag convoy had pulled in to a rest stop in nowheresville South Australia a few weeks back and there he was, sitting on his tattered backpack by the kerb outside Hungry Jack's, talking to himself while grinning like a loon and puffing on a rollie. I dropped Steph off and chucked a uey so I could drive up beside him.

I lowered the window and said, 'Hey, mate, you need a ride?'

It took him a few seconds to notice me. His hands were trembling. He had cuts on his face and the beginnings of a shiner. Someone had worked him over pretty good.

'You with the circus?' he asked.

He was in the back seat when Steph returned with the burgers. I had to ask her to go back in and get something for him. The kid was hungry, dirty and desperate—just what I was looking for.

We were two hands down after a bad night in Mount Gambier when Diego had got himself arrested and Karen, the attendant on the Cyclone, had declared her undying love for some local boy out of the blue. Even though she'd only been out with him three times she said she was going to stay and be the mother of his child. She hadn't even missed her period yet (I found this out later from Steph) but claimed she just *felt* pregnant. She was better off than Diego, at any rate. He had fake ID and no work visa so he was probably lounging in a detention centre somewhere in the middle of the fucken desert by now.

I'd worked the Kingdom long enough to know that's how things went. I'd seen my fair share of weary people by the side of the road and behind the counter in diners and out the back of bars. They were all looking for a way out of their situation. There was romance in running off with a travelling carnival, no doubting that, but whatever illusions these people held were soon shattered by long hours on the road and constant abuse from the inevitably unsatisfied public.

Most of them didn't last a season, eloping during the night with some newfound lover promising richer horizons, or succumbing to old habits—stealing or drinking or shooting up on their breaks. Some wound up in prison. Families or bad debts caught up with others. A few got religion and were politely asked to move on when their preaching became too much for the rest of us to bear. Once in a while someone got mangled by a ride thanks to a moment's inattention, or knifed between the ribs by some aggrieved local.

Target Ball lay at the unpopular end of sideshow alley, far from the glittering lights of the big rides. I needed some manic kid to run the stall for me while I tended to business, and Mikey seemed like the sort of young fella I could just about put up with for the summer. I supposed he'd flit on out of there eventually, like all the rest. He took a shine to me straightaway, and I suppose I liked him well enough at first too.

He wasn't really that much younger than me, at least not in years. He reminded me of guys I served with, except they toted real weapons to back up their gangster talk. Just as well nine mils weren't available to young blokes in Australia. There'd be no men aged fourteen to thirty left standing. The dickheads would all shoot each other.

'What's these lyrics for?' I asked Mikey. 'The same song you were working on back in South Australia?'

'Which one was that?' He had this way of blinking really fast when he was thinking about something. It made him look like he was having a seizure.

I thought back to those frantic first few hours in the car after we picked him up, when he wouldn't shut up. 'I don't know, some shit about golf?'

Mikey closed his eyes tight and sucked his bottom lip in under his top front teeth, which were amazingly still intact, no mean feat for a mouthy kid like him.

Take out ya service firearm, point it at my head
You a mean muthafucka like Stallone as Judge Dredd
'Cept that ain't Cristal, fool, that's jus' sparklin'
  wine
The golf course is the closest you ever been to a nine.

I clicked my fingers and nodded. 'Yeah, that's the one. This the same song?'

'Look, for a start they're not really what you'd call songs, a'ight? They's tracks, and a lyricalist like me, you just gotta keep on coming up with fresh rhymes until you gots enough to make a mixtape.'

'A tape? No one listens to tapes anymore, do they?'

'Nah, man, it's just a figure of speech. A mixtape's like a, like a digital playlist, y'know, a mix of tracks that an artist puts together so's producers can get an idea of their style and what have you. All you needs is some sick beats and mad skills on Garage Band and you're pretty much set. Plus a quality mic, obv.'

'Obv. And a shitload of lyrics.'

'Now you're feelin' me. That's why I'm out here, on the road with you and all the other freaks in the motherfuckin' Kingdom. No offence.'

'None taken. I seem to remember being the one who hired you.'

'Gots to earn me some chedda so's I can bankroll my rise to power. An' draw some inspiration from all the weird shit that goes on round here.'

'Every battle needs a stratagem.'

'A whatagem?'

'It's from *The Art of War*. Sun Tzu.'

'Wait, was he in the Wu Tang Clan?'

'Yeah, not quite. It's an old book a lot of soldiers read.'

'Oh, righto. Gives you advice on tactics and shit?'

'Something like that. Anyway, you're not earning any *chedda* standing round talking to me while all these punters are walking right on past the stall. Let's see you put those lyrical skills to good use and make us both some cash money.'

'I got your six, boss man. Stand back and marvel as I explain the rules of engagement to these Whisky Tango motherfuckers.'

His propensity for mixing the military jargon he'd heard from me in with his hippity-hop nonsense was unsettling, but he told me lots of rappers did it. I took his word for it. Some of the lingo he used, though...I asked him one time how a grommet from Freo like him ever learned the word 'erudite', after he dropped it in one of his verses. I didn't even know what it meant. His explanation was that despite hip-hop's roots in the ghetto (I laughed at that) MCs often had excellent vocabularies, as they were always listening out for interesting words to make rhymes. They didn't necessarily have to understand what they meant, or use them in the correct context.

'Syntactical assimilation, dawg,' he'd said. 'Hip-hop makes you smarter! It's an education from the streets, you feel me?'

I didn't, not really, but I let it slide, half suspecting he was better educated than he was letting on.

I picked at a sliver of wood on the counter as Mikey launched into showman mode, the blue streaks of his pumped veins forming pipelines across his skinny biceps. He hiked up his pants and adjusted the laces on his Nikes, folding them carefully away behind the tongue. He took off his cap and readjusted his thick mop of greasy curls, a faint line of soft stubble above his mouth visible under the downward lights of the stall.

'Laydeez an' gentlemen, brothers an' sisters, friends an' enemies, lookee here now an' try your luck at the easiest game on sideshow alley. Win a prize for the kiddlywinks! Three balls for a dollar, eight for two bucks! How 'bout you, sir, you look like you've got the equipment to lob one in the hole from fifty yards away! Win a giant panda for the little lady? They's an endangered species, y'know. Only three thousand left in the world, an' that's the triple truth!'

The generator spluttered, so I gave it a little encouragement with my boot. A puff of dust kicked up from the casing and settled back down on the vibrating metal as it resumed its drone. I leaned back on my chair to watch the crowd.

It was a hot evening and the smell of fairy floss and horse sweat hung in the air. I craned my neck forward to look up at the sky. The stars were hidden behind a low ceiling of cloud. Rain was on the way.

2

The crowd was slow: mostly bored women dragging slouching kids and unemployed husbands around the stalls. It wasn't exactly what you'd call a carnival atmosphere, and the crews all looked irritated. The prospect of making any money was slight—everyone knew it. After a while you learn how to spot it, the pinched lips of sinewy locals cruising past. Lot lice, we called them.

None of the hands tried drawing them in with a bit of ballyhoo. There was no point. No money and nowhere else to go. The kids would stare at the shiny rides with their hollowed-out eyes and occasionally risk a pleading stare at their fathers. The men would gaze into the middle distance, giving a shake of the head.

Trouble usually started just after nine, and sometimes it would be indirectly my fault, not that anyone knew. I was always careful not to give the other stallholders any reason to start a beef with me. Although my customers were far from reliable, they also depended upon me and I had made it clear that anyone who brought hassle to my joint would be cut off. I reckon most of them feared that more than anything else. They could take a hiding but if their meth supply dried up, well, that didn't bear thinking about.

For the most part, trouble on the show came courtesy of a more socially acceptable drug: booze. My customers usually couldn't muster the energy for scrapping, unless they were short on cash and desperate. They'd just take their glass home and smoke it up there. The further away from me, the better, as far as I was concerned.

As for the others, the drunks and pill poppers, the speed freaks, you could spot them a mile off. Over the course of the evening their weather-beaten faces would begin to melt. The corners of their mouths would droop. Their squinty eyes would widen at the dizzying array of lights and colours on the alley. Driven mad by obnoxious dance music (I sympathised on that front) and the gradual emptying of their already-thin wallets, some of these local blokes would make an earnest start on the activity they had really come to the show for.

It wasn't just the men. At least once a night a couple of women would go at it too, and I'm not talking handbags at twenty paces. These fights were brutal scrapes that always ended with someone spitting up blood. People hate each other in these godforsaken places.

Two coppers passed by Target Ball, half-eaten pies in one hand, the other hovering near holstered pistols. They had that look about them: small-town lawmen who knew they might have to draw down on someone before the night was out. They seemed oblivious to the noisy family crowd, accustomed to disregarding it, picking up on what was happening just out of sight. They stared in the direction of the Cyclone, but that was an unlikely spot for a brawl. The pushing and shoving usually took place in the dustbowl surrounding the main attractions, visible enough for spectators but at a safe distance from any families.

I leaned out of the stall to follow the cops' haphazard progress, their calm voices parting the crowd. *'Scuse me, miss. Step aside, please, mate.*

Whatever shambolic wrestling took place would be quickly broken up, and the participants moved on or taken into custody by coppers who knew them. They might spend a night in the cells if the sergeant deemed them too pissed to return to their wives. Matters only took a nasty turn if the cops sided with the aggressor, maybe through bitterness at the mess the show inevitably brought to town. If a discreet payoff didn't do the trick, we'd all be up at dawn the next day to break down the rides and strike camp.

No one wanted that. It rarely happened, though. There was always some copper willing to take the juice. It's the fucken Wild West out here.

Shrieking sounds coming from the Ghost Train were

par for the course but the way the two roaming coppers accelerated towards them told me a fight had broken out over spilled drinks or a poorly timed wink at someone else's girl or some old grudge. The crowd surged, eager to witness two blokes pummelling each other.

I stayed put. In Echuca, two men with handguns had robbed Shark Bites during a scuffle. It all happened in seconds. By the time Delia had alerted Ronnie, who'd just stepped out to see what was going on, the thieves were long gone. Ronnie was furious that his missus had been braced and the night's takings pocketed. He'd scoured the alley for an hour afterwards, clutching a crowbar, ready to stove in the skull of anyone who so much as looked askance at him.

The coppers returned five minutes later, escorting two young men in handcuffs. The prisoners were clearly a little worse for wear, their eyelids drooping and feet struggling. One guy was bleeding from the corner of his mouth and tried to spit as he passed by our stall, a pathetic dribble of blood and saliva trailing from his puffy lips. The other's right arm was exposed, the sleeve of his shirt torn away in the fight. One of his eyes was closing up fast, pink and swollen where it had encountered a fist or an elbow.

Normal service quickly resumed. The unscheduled entertainment for the evening was over, at least for the time being. I wondered if the fella with the messed-up eye managed to clock the legend carved into the wooden beam over the entrance to our section of the carnival. *In the Kingdom of the Blind, the One-eyed Man is King.*

As the crowd began to disperse, I saw one of my regulars hovering by Shark Bites. I hadn't seen him since the last time we'd come through these parts and I hardly recognised him. His cheeks were sunken and his hair had thinned badly. His gaunt figure was drowning in a hoodie that had probably once fitted him. He obviously wasn't going to be a customer much longer.

He gave me a questioning nod and I realised he was reluctant to approach because of Mikey. There'd been someone else working the stall last time. I nodded that it was okay.

'Take five,' I told Mikey.

'I'm a'ight, boss, I already had a break.'

'Smoko. Go on.'

Mikey sucked air in through his teeth, glancing between me and the guy in the hoodie shuffling his way through the crowd. He said nothing but I knew he'd most likely worked it out by now, or at least suspected something. I unlocked the door and let him out. He sniffed, hiked his jeans, pulled a crumpled ciggie from his top pocket and wandered off, though not too far.

I handed the guy in the hoodie a plastic bucket with five tennis balls.

He slipped me a fifty-dollar note.

'That'll buy you a point,' I told him.

'Any change?' he muttered.

'Nah. But if you land three of those balls in one of the hoops, I'll give you a bonus point.'

'For reals?'

'It's all in the wrist. Let's play.'

He gulped and tried to concentrate, but his first throw didn't even make the backboard. It hit the lower edge and rolled under the counter.

'Make a fucken effort,' I growled.

His next two balls at least hit the main board, but then he was done. He stared dejectedly down at the two remaining balls.

I reached for one of the blue koalas on the top shelf and handed it to him. 'Congratulations, sir, you've won a prize. Thanks for playing and do come again.'

He attempted to smile. His teeth were black and rotten. Off he went, clutching his cuddly koala. I added the fifty to my roll as Mikey flicked his ciggie away and came back to the stall, wearing a shit-eating grin.

'Getting generous there, boss, giving away prizes to chumps.'

'Don't miss much, do you?'

'I know not to hand out those blue koalas to the kiddly-winks.'

'See that you don't.'

I retreated to my seat at the back and watched him throw down some bally for the marks. He had a way of intriguing the ladies (there was a tiny bit of handsome hidden underneath that fake-gangster exterior) and goading the men just enough that they would want to prove themselves. Sometimes he flirted too obviously with the women and infuriated the blokes, but seeing him in action the past few weeks I'd become convinced he could handle blue-koala duties, which would free me up to visit the labs and step up production. He was the best prospect I'd seen in a long time. Also, he was the only prospect.

If you want to build an operation, you need competent soldiers. You don't have to trust them. In fact, you'd be stupid to do so. You just have to know the limits of their abilities. Same thing in the army. I might've made colonel if I'd stayed in. It pissed me off how they treated me at the end, but it was tactical experience that I was now putting to good use.

The crowd thinned out as the evening wore on, and Mikey counted the poke. He'd made good money at a time when there wasn't much cash floating around, but the constant interaction with chumps had left him ragged. There were big sweat patches on his Freo shirt. I broke open a bottle of water and handed it to him.

'Man, there were so many bona-fide white-trash puckered-up *assholes* in tonight, I can hardly fucken believe it. I mean, what's the asshole-to-normal-Joe ratio in these towns? S'gotta be three to one, maybe four. And the skanks circling those assholes? Jesus, Mary and Joseph, brother, why'd you wanna be orbitin' brown stars like those guys? Dock your titty starship in my space station, princess, knowwhumsayin'? Tractor beam *engaged*.'

He always said 'asshole' instead of 'arsehole', which annoyed me. Another American affectation. As if I didn't hear enough of that whiny shit in the service. I noticed his hands were shaking as he gulped the water. There was definitely something wrong with the kid. Probably should be on medication for hyperactivity.

'That's the job,' I said as he handed me the evening's sticky takings.

'It's okay for you sittin' in back, nobody's gettin' on your case all night, asking for free shit and where's the dunnies and I want to make a complaint 'cos my daughter got sick after riding the Cyclone. So what the fuck you let her on it for after stuffing a large pepperoni pizza, three Cokes and half a fucken kilo of fairy floss into her Jabba the fucken Hutt pie hole?'

'I worked this stand a long time, Mikey. People give me shit too.'

'Yeah, not for very long though, huh? You just give 'em that look and they crap their pants and step the fuck off.'

'I've got a look?'

'Go check yourself out in the hall of mirrors, dawg... Hey, lift your shirt and show me your tatt again.'

'What for?'

'Just do it, a'ight? I've been thinkin' of gettin' one.'

'Not like this, I hope.'

I'd made the mistake of showing him my battalion tattoo that first day in the car. He'd told me his pop had been in the military but flunked out.

I glanced around to make sure no one was watching and rolled up my right sleeve. The tattoo was of a snarling blue heeler. The Sixth Battalion motto, *Duty First*, was etched underneath the slobbering hound.

Mikey stared at it, rocking back on his heels. 'Fucken awesome. Does everyone in the Bluedog get one of them?'

'Pretty much. You've been keeping it to yourself like I told you, right?'

He slid a forefinger and thumb across his mouth. 'I know you don't want no dumb-ass questions.'

'No more'n usual, if I can help it.'

I rolled my sleeve back down, rueing that I'd ever shown him the tatt. Must have been desperate to recruit him.

The chumps were still filing slowly out of the alley, which would take half the night to clean up, bins overflowing with takeaway wrappers and tinnies, not a pretty sight.

I knew some of the crew were planning to head into Wodonga proper and go on the tear. These outings rarely ended well for the carnival hands, though it depended on the bar and how much the locals had lost that day. It was not usually a great idea to throw money around on booze if you'd just taken it out of the pockets of the people sitting in the same establishment, as a rule of thumb.

'You comin' for a drink?' Mikey asked. 'Or you gonna release the hounds on Steph tonight? Man, that be one fine figure of a lady you got there, that girl got some *grounds*, knowhumsayin'?'

'I'd tell you to watch that mouth of yours, but it wouldn't make any difference, would it?'

'Probs not,' he grinned. 'Come on, boss, come have a brewski with me, maybes we can talk some *bidness*.'

The little shit had the jump on me. Have to always watch your six. I nodded and dangled the keys to my ute. He snatched them out of my fingers and began to sing the Dockers' club song. *Oh Freo, give 'em the old heave-ho!*

3

The sight of so many utes in the car park of the Pumphouse was reassuring. I directed Mikey to a spot where we wouldn't be hemmed in if we had to get out in a hurry. The bar would be raucous and packed with farm workers, many of them itinerant. Hopefully we could blend in. It wasn't like the piano player would stop mid-tune and everyone would turn to stare at us, although you never knew with some of these fucken shit-kicker places.

Once inside, I elbowed my way through a crowd of flannel shirts to find a rickety table at the far end of the room, close to the toilets and within sight of what you might call a dance floor, if you had a vivid imagination. A trio of heavily made-up local girls were doing the Melbourne two-step around their gaudy handbags. Half a dozen men in tight jeans were cradling pots while checking them out. A Lady Gaga song was straining the speakers. I couldn't tell you which one—they all sound the fucken same.

Mikey headed straight to the bar and squirmed back a few minutes later balancing several rounds of drinks. He had his fingers inside the necks of four beer bottles, some cheap European shit I'd never heard of that was on special. Once it touched your lips, you understood why. He was cradling a couple of shots, which I grabbed before he lost his grip and added to the stains on his shirt.

I didn't like the look on his face, a mixture of disgust and wide-eyed excitement. 'Is this a fucken fag joint, or what?' he shouted, loud enough that I noticed at least four men glaring in our direction.

'None of them in towns like this,' I told him, sipping the beer and wishing I'd gone to the bar instead of sending him. 'At least not that anyone would cop to, anyway.'

'Yeah, right, you notice the music and the name of the place? I rest my case, your honour.'

'The girls seem to be enjoying it.'

Mikey turned in his seat to survey the dance area, shaking his head in despair.

'Yo, the gaylords from Duran Duran called, ladies,' he shouted, one hand up to his ear as if accepting a phone call, 'they want their fucken eyeliner back.' He turned back to me, cackling. 'Man, you seein' this train wreck of fashion here? It's like this place got caught in a time warp or somethin'.

What a fucken travesty. By the time this town catches on to the hip-hop revolution, we'll be flyin' round on jetpacks an' shit.'

I pinched the bridge of my nose between forefinger and thumb. 'Fuck sake, Mikey, you're going to get us kicked out of this place in record time. At least let me drink this awful piss first.'

Mikey flicked a bony hand at me and gulped back a shot of whisky. 'A'ight, a'ight, don't sweat it, boss man, the Gaga's too loud, they can't hear for shit.'

It wasn't entirely true but I nodded reluctant assent and leaned back in my chair. I scanned the room for other hands from the show, yet I couldn't spot anyone I recognised. There were so many people jammed into the small space that they could have been standing ten feet away and I wouldn't have noticed. The dance floor was now obscured by a forest of thin denim legs. They'd start fucken line dancing in a minute, I just knew it.

The beer tasted rank but it was hot in there, so I drank it anyway. Mikey skolled two bottles and both of his shots in the time it took me to reach the suds at the bottom of my first. He screwed up his face in disdain as he watched the ruddy farm boys dance with the local fillies. Flushed, curvaceous blondes dressed in shiny boots and sequined shirts linked arms with young blokes who looked like they wouldn't be out of place on the back of a horse in the 1950s. The music seemed to be getting worse, somehow.

'Who's this?' I asked Mikey, pointing up at the ether.

'Miley Cyrus.' He grimaced.

'Your Fifty Cent diss was worse than I thought.'

I watched his Adam's apple bobbing as he poured the last of the beer down his gullet, eyes half closed. I decided to talk business before he was too far gone to take in my proposal.

'About the blue koalas.' I leaned in close across the table. It was hard to hear yourself think when Billy Ray's daughter was wailing in your ears.

'You needs to freshen up the prizes on that stall, dawg, the kiddlywinks want something more innerestin than friggen native roadkill. Fuck those wombats an' shit, how 'bout we gets some giraffes or rhinos or pythons—yeah, some snakes, man, that'd be dope!'

'I'm trying to offer you a job, dickhead.'

Either he couldn't hear, or he was wilfully ignoring me. He cupped a palm over one ear, making headphones, and scratched an imaginary record on the table with the first two fingers of his other hand.

> *Join up wit NASA an' fly to Venus*
> *Read da news on TV like Anton Enus*
> *Run away wit da circus like Bailey an' Barnum*
> *Or become a rock singer like Johnny Farnham*

He threw both hands in the air, jumped up from his seat and turned three-sixty, flinging his arms around to whatever mysterious rhythm burned inside his head.

'Woo! You cop a look at the titties on some of these biatches? Pure corn-fed country home cookin' that is, sitting

28

up nice and perky for all these goggle-eyed motherfuckers to leer at.'

'Calm down, will you? Have a drink, you fucken loon.'

'I'm out. Needs me a clip for my nine.'

'Take one of these. I don't want to wrap the ute round a tree anyway.'

He sat down and gunned the remaining shots one after the other before starting on the last beer. I could see where this was going. I made a mental note to prop his head out the window on the way back. It was a long drive to the next town on the schedule.

Two fairly pretty cowgirls passed by our table then, heading in the direction of the bathroom. They smiled at me, preened their hair and glanced back in my direction. It was too dark to see my neck, obviously.

'Shee-it, did you see that, homie? You got somethin' those two hornbags want real bad, boss man.'

'Fuck off, Mikey.'

'I's just sayin', a big muscly army motherfucker like you, gym body an' all, probs got a schlong like a baby's arm. You gots to take advantage of nature's gifts, dawg. Be criminal to pass up an invite like that.'

My patience had just about reached its limits. 'I'm going for a piss. If you don't want to walk home to the Kingdom, cut this shit out when I get back. I wanted to talk business.' His idiotic way of talking was so infectious, I almost said 'bidness'.

'Oh, I see, y'all are going after those two to bang 'em

in a stall, huh?'

It wasn't until I stood up that I realised how much I had been sweating. I couldn't tell if Mikey was trying to get a rise out of me or if he was just a muppet incapable of keeping his trap shut.

It was quieter in the men's, though bursts of music blared in every time someone opened the door. A couple of locals looked me up and down as I pissed but they didn't speak to me. I took my time washing my hands and splashed some water over my head. The roadmap of scars on my neck looked red and angry under the dim lights of the bathroom. The cool drops running through my hair felt good.

I shook myself off and stood up straight, smoothing my shirt and yawning. The night was a washout. Mikey would fall over drunk soon, and I'd have to drag him back to the Kingdom.

When I returned to our table two other men were sitting there, sipping beers and surveying the dance floor.

'My friend and I are sitting here,' I told them.

Heads swivelled to stare at me. The younger one had a wispy moustache. 'Don't look that way to me, mate,' he said.

I ignored him, scanning the crowd for a sign of Mikey. I assumed he was embarrassing himself somewhere out on the dance floor, probably gyrating up against someone's girlfriend while imploring her to 'shake her booty'.

A young bloke clad head to toe in denim emerged from the crowd, his blond hair combed neatly down. He made a beeline for me and raised a hand in cautious greeting.

It took me a second or two before I recognised him as a mark who'd come round the stall asking about crystal. One of my established clients had recommended he talk to me. After I'd checked him out, I'd given him a free sample. I knew he'd be back.

'Paul, right?'

He was surprised I remembered his name.

'Yeah. Look, I hope you don't mind me coming over like this, but your mate's in strife.'

'Why, where is he?'

'Couple of boys took him out the back.'

'Say what now?'

'I don't know, mate, I think he was mouthing off. They frogmarched him out of here so fast his feet hardly touched the ground.'

'Appreciate it, Paul.'

'Yeah, but you might want to...'

I pushed my way through the crowd towards the door, leaving Paul in my wake. It was warm outside, and I stood by the entrance for a moment to get my bearings and adjust to the sudden quiet. Like I'd done a thousand times in the desert, I slowed my breathing and listened to the night. Behind the curtain of cicadas and drone of the highway I could hear the distinctive muffled sounds of a fight.

I stepped to the corner of the pub and the noise increased. I saw them then, three men standing over Mikey. He was trying to get up as they put the boot in. They were only twenty metres away, partially obscured by a large flatbed ute. I broke into a run, with no intention of stopping until I collided with them.

Two of the assailants looked up as I approached. I swear my feet were gliding over the gravel like I was fucken ice skating. It was beautiful. They tried to move back and ready themselves for me, but I was in juggernaut mode. I spared a glance down at Mikey—I couldn't tell how badly he was hurt, and maybe that was just as well.

I changed tack at the last second, veering away from the two men who'd spotted me. Instead, I shoulder charged the heavyset guy who was kicking Mikey's curled-up body. The impact knocked him clean off his feet and into the passenger door of the ute. His elbow smashed the side window and he slid down in shock, a big gash opening up on his forearm. I wheeled on the other two, throwing a few quick, wild punches, windmilling to make them back off. One of them panicked a bit and flailed his arms madly to avoid me. The lucky prick caught a hold of my shirt and clung onto it as he stumbled and fell to his knees.

As I tried to pull away from him the third guy whacked me on the temple with his fist, a dull thud made worse by the three gold rings across his knuckles. Given his fat friend had a handful of my shirt, my only option was to scrape the edge of my boot down his shinbone and stomp on his foot as hard as I could.

I tell you what, not many people can stand the pain of having their shin kicked or scraped. It's fucken white-hot pain, just blots out everything. The bloke sucked in a huge breath and his eyes rolled back in his head. His lips parted to expose two rows of shining, pristine teeth. I couldn't resist. I elbowed him hard in the mouth and felt a couple of those pretty little babies crumble. He staggered back and spat a plume of blood, roaring in pain as he clutched his mashed-up lips. He fell heavily, a great cloud of dust billowing up with the weight of the cunt.

In the absence of any other weapon, the overweight bloke on the ground sank his teeth into my thigh. I clenched so fast I bit my tongue, bringing the metallic taste of blood to my mouth. I lashed out at the guy's face with my heel and felt a cheekbone give way, though it might have been an eye socket. The bloke opened his jaws and turned white before passing out. As he crumpled to the ground my shirt ripped right down the back, along the seam. I thrashed around, trying to wriggle out of it. Still curled up in the dirt, Mikey moaned and squirmed out of the way of it all.

I was so busy untangling myself I only caught a glimpse of the first man as he pile-drove into me. We went down together, his bulk slamming me into the dirt. The prick was all over me. He stank of whisky and cheap cologne. Blood poured out of the cut on his forearm and smeared over my chest as he sat astride me, raining down blows.

My arms were free so I went into a defensive boxing position as best I could, but he still landed a few corkers on my neck and around my ears. I knew if I didn't get up I'd be in trouble soon. I tensed my spine against the ground, assessing his weight.

I sat up quickly and headbutted him in the solar plexus. That knocked the breath out of him. He let out a great wheeze and froze for a second, his fists opening and closing reflexively with the shock of it.

I slipped my arm under one of his thighs and used my momentum to flip him off me. As we pivoted I drove my knee into the small of his back, just above the third vertebrae. He flung his arms out over his head, letting out four short gasps. I went to one knee and stood up, shaking my head to clear it as he rolled over.

He had one hand on his spine as if he was trying to hold it together. He raised the other in deference.

'Wait, stop, stop, that's enough—Christ, my fucken back, you've broke me fucken back.'

He shuffled away from me, terrified he was paralysed. In the back of my mind I was thinking, Fuuuck, this is not good. I held off, dropping my hands to my knees and bending over to catch a breath. The other two blokes weren't going anywhere anytime soon.

Three big blokes. I'd been lucky. They could've been toting a shiv, or worse. I composed myself, tapping into the adrenaline rush.

'You better not have hurt the young fella,' I warned the last one, who stopped writhing around after he worked out his back was not permanently damaged.

Still holding his hands outwards in a placatory gesture, he rose haltingly to one knee, wincing and closing his eyes tight with the pain.

I waited to see what he was going to do next. Eventually he opened his eyes and breathed out.

'Fuck me, mate. That was a Muay Thai move. You could've fucken killed me.'

'Didn't see you holding back.'

My shirt was hanging in tatters from one arm. He took in my infantry tattoo, then the burn scars on my chest and neck. He looked down and swore under his breath.

'I don't fucken believe it. You serve?'

I nodded. 'Uruzgan.'

'For fuck sake. We're at the logistics base in Wodonga. You in the Bluedog?'

I shrugged apologetically.

'Christ all fucken mighty. Your prick of a mate there's lucky to have you on his side.'

He was in good shape but I knew if he was at the logistics base he'd never seen any action. I clocked him swallowing the fear that had suddenly formed in his throat, his surprise at its unfamiliar taste.

'We done here?' he said.

'I am if you are. Best see to the chubby guy. He doesn't look too good.'

'Fat prick. Almost got my back broke over nothing.'

I stared at him a little longer, taking note of his stance, waiting to see if he was bluffing. The only sounds came from the man with the smashed mouth, who was in the foetal position, whimpering a woman's name over and over.

'I'm sorry, May. I'm sorry.'

35

I stretched my jaw, satisfied the recruit was not going to recommence hostilities now he knew where I'd been.

'May his missus?' I asked.

'Nah, his wife's called Jess.' He stood up slowly, bending his back, eyes bulging. 'Must be his dentist.'

4

The smoke parted around me to reveal an enormous crater in the road, scattered with debris and the remains of people turned inside out. In the middle of the hole lay the husk of what had once been a camouflaged Humvee. It was scorched black and burning now, upside down on its roof. Oil and blood oozed from the crushed cab, mingling to form a sticky goop.

Deafened by the explosion, I stumbled down into the crater and immediately regretted it. The first thing I saw was a single boot sitting in the dirt. Jutting up from inside it was a jagged red shinbone. I stared dumbly, knowing what it was yet unable to process the information. My stomach started doing somersaults.

Next to the boot was the head and upper body of Sergeant Ludowyk. Her right arm and legs were nowhere to be seen, and her lower jawbone was hanging by a gory thread of flesh. I stood there, gawping at the charred corpse of my friend for five uncomprehending seconds and then I was in the air, knocked off my feet by a second impact that I didn't even hear.

I came down next to the thing that had once been Paulina Ludowyk and rolled onto my side so I didn't have to look anymore. It felt like God had reached down and swatted me with his fist.

That's when I saw the second Hummer, the one I had just crawled out of, roll weirdly onto its side at the lip of the crater. It had been ripped down the middle by what could only have been a direct RPG hit. Maybe I was concussed, I don't know. I lay there in the muck, unable to move, watching it crumble like a tower of Lego knocked over by a kid having a tantrum. I couldn't look away.

One of the back wheels popped off the axle and pinged straight up in the air, the burning rubber leaving a trail of black smoke against the clear blue sky. The passenger-side door whooshed high over my head, a smoking frisbee. The whole thing happened in one second flat, maybe two, but every detail was clear.

The fuel tank ignited then and a beautiful orange jet of flame blossomed outwards, reaching down to caress me. I scrabbled feebly back in the dirt. The fire loomed over me like a phoenix finally freed from its egg. Then it fell upon me, claws tearing at my flesh.

I jerked awake, slick with sweat. Instinctively I placed a palm on my chest and concentrated on slowing my breathing. The scar tissue was hot to the touch, tender. I traced the raised lines with my fingertips.

Steph was next to me, splayed on her back, one arm over her head clutching at the pillow. There was a faint patch of stubble in her armpit and her face was partially obscured by her mop of blonde hair. She was dead to the world, a ragdoll. Once she was out, you practically had to spray her with a hose to wake her.

The sheets were a tangle around Steph's knees, kicked off in the night. It had been a hot one. I took in her elongated body, and stroked the smooth burn mark on her hip. It was the only real blemish on her body—she complained about her arse, like most women I know, but I couldn't see a thing wrong with it. Her burn had been obtained in less dramatic fashion than mine, while ironing in the nude, long before we met.

She didn't stir, even when I let my fingertips skate over the skin of her belly to the top of her trimmed pubic hair. She kept it short in summer and grew it out as winter approached, then went back to a fuzzy strip or some other shape in spring (a downward pointing arrow one time—she isn't the subtlest of girls). I traced figure eights on the sharp bristles but she didn't register until I pressed further down. Then she exhaled and turned her head towards me, opening her eyes slowly and smiling, then closing them again.

'Morning,' she breathed.

'You awake?'

'I am now.'

I was going to tell her I'd had the dream again but she arched her back and reached across to start stroking my dick. It was how we began a lot of mornings, and as she made me come the lingering memories of the burning were banished.

After, as I stared up at the stains on the ceiling of her trailer, a dull pain began pulsing in my left ear and I remembered what had happened the night before.

I stood up gingerly, a series of aches becoming instantly apparent. I'd taken a few knocks, though nothing like what Mikey had copped.

I'd come to sleep with Steph after bedding him down in my trailer. I wouldn't normally let anyone other than Steph in there but I could hardly have taken him back to the communal bunks. Steph was still awake, just, and she had cleaned me up and rubbed one of her magic ointments into my arms and back. I don't know if it did any good, but I slept well enough after that and a couple of Panadeine Forte.

Mikey was badly shaken up. He was bleeding from the nose and mouth, but not so heavily as to suggest internal injuries. I'd seen that before—there was no mistaking a ruptured organ. His blood had mingled on my chest with that of the bloke I'd fought as I carried him across the silent alley, picking a path through abandoned fast-food wrappers and ticket stubs. He was even lighter than I thought he'd be, little more than a gangly teenager. I'd carried a couple of guys like that out of harm's way in Uruzgan too. Decent kids, but fucken useless. Incapable of taking care of themselves. There'd always be some twitchy young fucker like Mikey who ran the wrong way or forgot to duck. The trick was getting them cas-evac'd before they bled out. They made it half the time, more or less.

Mikey wrapped his quivering hands around my torso like he was trying to suckle at my tit. They'd really got stuck into him for whatever he'd said. And it was hard to believe he hadn't deserved it, to some degree. But no one ever steps in anymore to call a stop to a beating. Blokes just keep kicking until they hear something break and then it's emergency rooms, brain scans and half-hearted apologies blaming the piss or their mates for egging them on. Way I see it, if you're going to take it to that level, it had better be worth it. The guy better have raped your wife or murdered your daughter. Otherwise, just get a few digs in and then step the fuck off.

When I set Mikey down outside my trailer he couldn't stand up. He'd caught a few blows to the face that looked worse than they were. Nothing seemed broken. I figured a hot bath and a couple of day's rest would do the trick. Within a week he'd be bragging about the fight and showing off his bruises.

I put my arm around his shoulders and helped him inside, walking him to my bed. He slumped down on the doona, clutching his guts and moaning. I asked how he was feeling and I knew from his sarcastic reply that he wasn't that bad.

'A thousand f-f-fucken per cent, dawg.' He looked around

the room, taking in my spartan digs. 'Nice bunk.'

Even though it was hot he was shivering and I was worried he'd gone into shock. I took my old army swag out of the cupboard and unrolled it. He lay back on the bed, and let me take his sneakers and jeans off.

'Hey, no funny stuff,' he mumbled as I helped him into the sleeping bag. I didn't want him wrapped up in my sheets. He wasn't all that clean. His face was a mess, so I soaked a towel and wiped the blood off. Snug inside the swag, he finally stopped shivering and his eyes began to blink shut. Satisfied he was going to sleep, I grabbed my wash kit and left, leaving the door unlocked so he could crawl outside and piss if he needed to. I hoped he wouldn't soil the bed.

I stood in the warm night air for a while after that, wondering what time it was. The light was still on in Steph's trailer so I tapped gently at her door, wincing at the pain in my knuckles. She was half asleep when she let me in, and didn't ask what had happened. She knew better.

I left Steph dozing in the crumpled sheets and padded to the front of her trailer to get a better look at my face in the make-up mirror she'd nailed over the breakfast bar. There were cuts on my cheekbones and bruises forming right across my brow. My eye sockets were dark and sunken. I dabbed at the wounds with a cloth, flinching each time.

I'd been lucky, Mikey even more so. I wondered what had happened to the three army trainees—if they had visited the emergency room, if coppers would come knocking at the door any minute now. The show was due to run a few more days in Wodonga. I really didn't need to spend that time banged up in the cells because I'd broken the teeth of some prominent local's favourite son.

A sharp pain flared up in my thigh and I stepped back to look at the bite. It was red and angry, despite Steph having dressed it with antiseptic. I took in my full reflection in the mirror. I looked like I'd been through the wars and I resolved to take it easy for a week or two, to spend more time being loved up by Steph, to avoid fraternising with Mikey and the other dedicated drinkers. There was a whole summer season to get through and I knew that if you sought out trouble in small towns, it would surely find you.

Steph's trailer was a mess. There were clothes scattered everywhere. Make-up and tiny bottles of essential oils were stacked haphazardly on every available surface, creating an overwhelmingly sharp scent that made my nostrils tingle. I peered back along the corridor. Steph snuffled and turned on her belly, her arse poking up in the air invitingly. She'd been telling fortunes and giving massages on the Kingdom for two years. I didn't buy into the palm reading but my scepticism didn't bother her. She'd been forgiving of my confronting appearance and I was grateful for that.

I drew a glass of water from the sink, pulled the curtain back and cracked open the window. The smell of breakfast cooking wafted in and my stomach growled. I found my pants and boots, then remembered I had no shirt. Everyone on the show knew about my burns but I didn't exactly enjoy parading around bare-chested if I could help it.

I went to Steph's wardrobe and pulled out her robe, a silky black number that was way too small for me. I liked it on Steph, though. It was a little short for her too, but I didn't mind that at all.

I opened the door to a bright morning sky, shielding my eyes from the silvery glare as I stepped down. The hatch at Shark Bites was open, and Delia was busying herself frying eggs and bacon on the grill. A few of the hands stood around conversing. I loped across to join them.

'Hey, Delia, can I get a couple of bacon and egg rolls?'

She looked me up and down and arched her eyebrows. 'You boys tie one on last night?'

'It wasn't too bad. I'm not hung, at least.'

'No need to be ashamed. Hey, Steph was up early. She off visiting her mum for a few days?'

That caught me off guard. 'Steph's still in bed.'

Delia threw her head back and guffawed, showing off the gaps in her teeth. Sweat trickled out from under her hairline. 'Ooh, think you better check on the identity of the young lady you're lying with, Ben Wallace. Steph lit on out of here at sparrow's. I was up answering the call and I seen her car pulling out. Get to my age and you're up five, six times a night. If I didn't know better I'd think I was with child but Ron had the snip a few years back so I don't see how that's possible.'

I stepped to the side of the stall to look down sideshow alley towards my trailer. Steph's old Datsun had been parked next to my ute. Sure enough, it wasn't there. I walked quickly, my mind racing. From twenty metres away I could see the door to my trailer was ajar. A sick feeling began to creep into my guts.

The bloodstained sleeping bag lay draped across the bed. My stuff was in disarray, scattered over the floor. I stood there for a minute, surveying the carnage.

The cigar box was upside down next to the nightstand. Motherfucker. I didn't think anyone would be able to find it, but he'd had all night, and I'd carried the fucken little fox right into the chicken coop. I bent down to retrieve the box, turning it over in my fingers before chucking it angrily into the corner. There had been close to ten thousand dollars in there, in fifties and a few hundreds. Nine thousand seven hundred, to be exact. All I'd saved in two weeks. I'd been meaning to drop it off at the storage unit once I hit ten grand. That was how I usually did things.

The money was Mikey's now, along with Steph's car. She'd probably left the keys in the ignition, as usual. He was gone, and he had half a night's start. Mother*fucker*. I pushed the stained swag off the bed and flopped down, staring at the bruises forming on my knuckles.

5

I'm not one of those hoons who thinks it's clever to rev at the lights and do burnouts. The SV6 is way too classy a machine for that. Dual overhead cammies, eighteen-inch alloy rims, and she takes corners like she's glued to the macadam. A lot of blokes say you've gotta go with a V8 but I took a spin in the SS and it was all over the place. You're just buying it for the sound of the engine. If you're a fucken idiot, that is. The SV6 was the first thing I got myself when the money really started coming in. Bottle green. Huge tray. Which is just as well, since I have to lug all Steph's stuff round with me now too. The Target Ball stand I just hook up to the towbar, but even with all the extra weight it's not a problem. You can tow a house with this rig.

If Mikey had taken it, well, Jesus. Different story entirely, I suppose. I'd have hired a couple of boys to hunt him down and bring him back to me, preferably in an unspecified number of pieces. As for the ten grand, I'd made that back in less than a week so I wasn't down much. Still, it was my money and I wanted it back, even if meth's going gangbusters in these small towns. I can hardly keep up with demand. New customers everywhere I go now.

Losing Steph's car was a pain too, but only a minor one. I'd promised her a new ride once we hit Queensland and she'd been scouring the pages of *Classic Cars* looking for a set of wheels that would fit her personality. Her words, not mine. Lately she'd been leaning towards an old Mustang, a '64 maybe, but it wasn't easy finding one that didn't have the arse ripped out of it and that also happened to be pink. She said red would do, at a pinch. I was more concerned at what was under the hood. A Mustang's all well and good until the fucken exhaust falls off in the middle of the Hume.

Steph was curled up in the passenger seat of the ute, a blanket pulled over her bare legs because I had the aircon pumping. It was only gone ten and already thirty-something degrees. Running in convoy was the easiest way for the Kingdom to travel and we were down the back behind the big trucks, cruising along on some quiet B road, about ten ks under the speed limit. Steph had her iPod plugged into the dash and was playing her usual repetitive trance stuff. I kept turning the volume down so it didn't do my head in, and periodically she'd lean forward and turn it back up again.

She'd dragged me to a bush doof two years before and then vanished for half the night. I wasn't into the sounds but I'd brought a couple of grams of glass with me and was that ever a good call. Drove out of there the next day with three grand in my pocket. Heard two guys jumped in the river and got impaled on sunken branches, another went missing. He turned up a week later, wandering in the wilderness. Fucken dickhead.

I was glad to be out of there, sick of being hugged by pilled-up hippy chicks with hairy pits. A couple of them were running around topless—that was all right, though it made me squirm to see those nipples getting toasted. Sore in the morning, I reckon. I only got into one spill with a bloke, who made some offhand smart-arse comment about my neck. His mates all just stood there while I bashed him, pissing in their fluoro fisherman pants. They even apologised for him after. Rainbow Serpent's no fucken Summernats, that's for sure. Put a beating on someone there and five minutes later you're in a full-on mêlée trying to avoid a stubby to the face.

It was pretty quiet country, farmland mostly, much of it unused. Occasionally there'd be a field of cane but we weren't really far enough north for it to amount to anything. Mostly it was just dry, empty pastures, galahs screeching past, a silo now and then. We could have been anywhere in Australia.

'You know, Mikey's not that different to the women who come in for card readings.'

'Get your feet off the dash.'

She did what I asked, but I knew I'd have to tell her again in a minute.

'Head full of crazy ideas, all fantasy and expectation. The vast majority of people coming in wanting their fortunes told have already decided what they want the cards to say. Nobody wants to hear that hard times lie ahead, or that sorrow will enter their lives, or financial difficulties, or that they will never find true love. It's weird—so many people buy into fantasies that have no relation whatsoever to their everyday reality. They expect some sort of hero narrative, or a family narrative, or worst of all a fucken *princess* narrative, and if it doesn't turn out that way they're unhappy and angry and disappointed.'

'Would do my head in.'

'God, tell me about it. They blame me if it's not all roses and champagne. Like somehow I can map out their futures for them. They want me to reassure them that they're doing the right thing, that they're on the correct path, that it will all work out for the best in the end. Thing is, though, the cards don't lie.'

'But you do.'

'Yeah. Course I do, as much as it pains me. You can't tell people the truth. That's not what they've paid to hear. They'd rather exist in a fantasy version of themselves. Just like your little friend Mikey.'

'He's no friend of mine.'

'That's why you and I get on so well, I reckon. We know what we are. We don't pretend to be anything else.'

'I don't know about that.'

'Yeah, totally. I mean, after what happened to you, it's not surprising.'

Steph reached across to touch my neck. I flinched, an automatic reaction.

'You don't live behind a façade, behind some sort of constructed personality. You're real, baby. You're authentic. There aren't many of us around.'

I had learned a long time ago not to question Steph's beliefs, even if I did think they were misguided. I usually just let her ramble on. It was easier that way. Less hassle. No point in picking a fight I couldn't win.

'I love the Zen state we exist in. People like us, we have a unique understanding of the world. We can see people for who they really are. It's not always nice. In fact it's frequently not nice at all, but that doesn't matter because we've got each other. It's you and me against the world, babe, and I'm in it with you till the bitter end.'

I appreciated the sentiment. I really did. It's not every woman that would have me. Such a load of bullshit, though.

Around 10.30 I spotted a car in the distance. As it approached I could see it looked like a blue Datsun, so I lifted my foot gently off the accelerator. Steph sat up straight when the vehicle behind sounded its horn at us for slowing down.

'What's wrong?'

'Hold on a sec. It's probably nothing.'

I was only doing forty ks an hour when the Datsun passed us in the opposite direction, so I was able to get a good look at the rego. I stepped on the brakes and steered in sharply to the hard shoulder. The car behind us roared past, its horn bellowing in protest. I watched the Datsun retreat in the side mirror and waited for the last two vehicles in the convoy to go past before I swung the wheel around and chucked a skidding uey. The Target Ball stand whipped around behind us and almost tipped. Finding the right side of the road again, I accelerated after the Datsun. The engine thrummed eagerly in response.

'Did you forget something?' Steph asked, her quizzical expression melting as the rear end of her car came into view.

'Oh. Well, good morning to you, old friend.'

It didn't take long to catch up to him. The Datsun was no match for the SV6. I had a bullbar so I thought, well, what's it for if not telling the car in front that you'd like a little chat? There was nobody else around. I edged forward until the ute touched the rear bumper of the Datsun. The driver floored it, pulling away from us again.

'Hey, don't damage the goods. I want that back in one piece.' Steph whacked me on the arm but I could tell she was enjoying this.

'Don't sweat it. We'll find you that Mustang you're after.'

'Very generous. What if he's not got the money with him and you need to find out where it is?'

I laughed and pressed on the accelerator. 'I'll interrogate him before I pull him out of the wreck.'

'And what if he doesn't survive?'

'Boo fucken hoo.'

He was never going to outrun me and I knew he would have little option but to pull over. All I had to do was give him a little encouragement, and if he didn't want to comply, well, that was fine by me. If he wanted to end his days mangled in a pile of burning, twisted metal, that was his choice, though I wouldn't recommend it as a way to go.

I gave him another nudge, a bit harder this time. The Datsun slewed across the lane but he managed to keep it on the road. There was nothing coming in the opposite direction, so I moved out beside him and allowed the steering to drag slowly to the left. He tried braking to get behind me but I anticipated that and slowed accordingly. With the trailer hitched, my vehicle was much longer than his and he was soon hemmed in. He drifted onto the hard shoulder and gave up, skidding down into an empty field and coming to a juddering halt in a cloud of dust.

I pulled over onto the verge and switched off the ignition. This was not dissimilar to how we used to force suspect vehicles off the road in the service. It usually ended badly, for them more often than us. My old reflexes kicked in and I was out of the cab and running through the grass to confront him before he had a chance to gather himself. To her credit, Steph wasn't far behind me as I yanked the Datsun's door open and reached inside to snatch a handful of the driver's T-shirt.

It wasn't Mikey. This guy was older, in his late thirties maybe. He had a ruddy country-boy face and was balding at the crown. The skin on his cheeks was pockmarked with old acne scars. He wasn't the town heart-throb, that was for sure. The striped polo shirt he was wearing had seen better days and his jeans had grease and food stains in the crotch. I dragged him out of the driver's seat and shoved him up against the side of the car. He struggled a bit but I could tell straightaway he was shitting himself.

'What? What?' he shouted, his voice trembling. 'What'd I do?'

I released his shirt, took a single step back and levelled a finger at his quivering jowls. 'Where is he?'

'Who? Who you after? Fucking hell, mate, take it easy.'

'The guy you got this car from.' I slammed my palm on the Datsun's roof next to his head, for effect. My anger was subsiding already. 'And don't tell me to take it easy. Now where is he? Answer carefully.'

The stranger blinked several times, shook his head and stammered, 'Nowra. He's in Nowra.'

'Friend of yours, is he?'

'Not really. He used to work out on my uncle's place. Why, what's he done?'

'Never you mind.'

Steph stepped forward, arms folded across her chest. 'Skinny little shit, yeah? Into hip-hop?'

The stranger snorted and relaxed a little. 'Uh, I don't think we're talking about the same person.' He exhaled and rolled his eyes. 'That's a relief. I thought...'

I wagged my finger menacingly in his face. 'Tell me exactly who gave you this car.'

The man winced. 'Old Bill Sherman—where else would I buy a car round here?'

'Uh huh. Keep talking.'

'Bill runs the scrappers down behind the servo. Bought this off him last week for three hundred bucks. It's not, uh, yours, is it?'

'Uh, yes, it *uh* is.' Steph made a face.

'Well, how was I supposed to know? I bought it from old Bill in good faith. Buggered if I know where he got it from.'

I turned away and kicked at a clump of dry grass. Not really what I'd hoped to hear, though I shouldn't have been surprised. I was dimly aware of the driver talking softly to Steph behind me, reassuring her that this was an honest mistake and that Bill Sherman was a decent old bloke, clearly not completely honest but not exactly a war criminal in hiding.

I wasn't much in the mood for that kind of bleating. I strode back and took hold of his T-shirt again, dragging him awkwardly onto the bonnet as he squealed in protest.

'This car was stolen from my girlfriend here, and the best you can do is this old fucken Bill shit?'

'What do you want from me?' he whined. 'I didn't do anything!'

'You're in receipt of stolen goods, for a start,' I said, and gripped the side of his head in my palm, grinding his cheek into the hot paintwork. He started making a huffing sound then and it was only when Steph touched me on the forearm that I realised he was crying.

It's just as well she intervened when she did. I was in the mood for leaving the guy with a couple of cracked ribs and a punctured lung for his trouble. Steph curled up her nose and shook her head, so I hoisted him back up onto his feet and bundled him away from the car. I hooked one foot around his ankle and shoved him so he fell on the grass.

When I looked back at the Datsun, Steph was already inside, her arse and feet poking out the door as she gathered whatever belonged to the driver and scooped it onto the ground. She took the keys from the ignition and went around to check the boot. There was a cardboard box full of stuff in there, so she dumped that into the field as well.

'That it?'

'I think so.' She rummaged in the boot a bit more and came out with her missing denim jacket, the one with the chequered lining that she wore often. She held it up, all smiles. 'Ha! Score! Glad he didn't chuck this.'

'Jump in,' I told her. 'Meet you back up on the road.'

She got into the car and adjusted the driver's seat, tutting as she pulled it forward. The rough terrain probably hadn't done wonders for the Datsun's chassis but as long as it made it to the next town we'd be all right. As far as I was concerned old Bill in Nowra would be fixing up any damage, not to mention providing me with every scrap of information he had on Mikey.

Steph gunned the Datsun back up the embankment, its rear wheels spinning momentarily on the grass. The driver was sitting up by then, hugging his legs, wisely holding his tongue. It was only when I turned to leave that he spoke.

'Mate, it's about thirty ks back into town. That's a long fucken walk.'

I halted and drummed my fingers against my thigh.

'So?'

'Well, give us a lift?'

I stepped back to where he was crouched and proffered my hand. He clutched my wrist, and as he rose I slapped him across the mouth with my free hand—so hard that it stung my palm. He let go of me and fell back to where he was sitting before, clutching his face.

Steph was waiting for me back on the road. I gave her the iPod from the ute and told her to stay in front of me just in case the Datsun carked it. She glanced at the bloke lying in the paddock and frowned at me, but said nothing.

'What? He asked for a lift. Can you believe that?'

'Oh.' She shook her head and grinned. 'I thought maybe he wanted his three hundred bucks back.'

'I'm not running a fucken charity.'

'I know, but, we did get the car back, baby, and my jacket.' She shrugged good-naturedly and raised an eyebrow.

'You're a soft touch.' I was annoyed by the situation but she was right, we had struck lucky. Although it was doubtful that this old Bill fellow would have the slightest idea where Mikey had gone, the morning had, on the whole, worked out better than anticipated. Now all I had to do was find the little prick, get my money back and explain to him why it was such a bad idea to cross me.

I rummaged around in the glove box until I found my wallet, counted six fifty-dollar notes from the roll and set off back down the embankment.

When he saw me coming the poor bastard scrabbled back in terror, one hand raised as a shield. He stopped when he spotted the pineapples. I threw them at him one after the other but decided to hold back on the last one. I slipped it into my jeans instead.

'Depreciation,' I told him. We left him there to count his losses.

6

Bill Sherman turned out to be a lot more useful than I'd anticipated. Not only did he tell me that Mikey had traded in the Datsun for a Commodore, securing the deal with a chunk of my money, but he also knew which way the bastard was headed. He even made me and Steph a cup of tea. I threw him a hundred bucks for the tip.

Bill told me that Mikey had gone out to Freddy McNamara's place to buy a shitload of meth. He hadn't even been subtle about it. Just asked Bill if he knew anyone selling crank in the area and was directed straight to Freddy's farm.

This set off plenty of alarm bells. Freddy was one of mine, running a lab out on his property inland from Nowra. Outside of Freddy and his crew, no one was supposed to know about the fucken place except for me. Someone had been flapping their lips, enough for a craggy old mechanic two towns over to hear about it.

As if that wasn't bad enough, I hadn't heard squat from Freddy, no phone calls, nothing. If Mikey had been out there looking to score, I should've known about it straightaway. The situation could have been wrapped up in no time. Instead, Freddy must have done a private deal and kept schtum. Fucken tweakers. You just can't get good staff these days. This was why I needed a reliable kid running the Target Ball stand—so I could attend to business properly.

Though it was hot I had the window down on the ute, my elbow resting on the doorframe. I flexed my hand and splayed my fingers open to catch the breeze as I barrelled down yet another country road. The bush round here all looks the same after a while but it's still pretty enough, if you're into that sort of thing. Endless fields, that indistinct heat shimmer at the horizon, all the foliage dry and yellow in contrast to the bitumen slicing right through it. Seeing it always made me imagine what it must have been like before the roads and railways came. I wondered what the nineteenth-century version of meth would have been— opium? That grew in fields, though at least you could process it in cities. The problem with meth is the almighty stench. You've got no other option but to go bush with your labs, but that's the beauty of it. No one ever goes there without a good reason.

The paddocks began to thin out as the road neared the

outskirts of Freddy's property. It was a nice spot. A copse of gums teeming with birds lay to the east. A drove of horses thundered down over the hill, thirty or forty in number, their flanks glistening in the morning heat, a plume of dust wafting in their wake. They wheeled as one, like a flock of birds, following the lead horse, slowing to a canter as they came over to watch my approach. I slowed down to get a look at them but the roar of the engine dropping a gear spooked them. They whinnied and galloped away from the fence, back towards the middle of the paddock for safety, the big stallion out front shaking his mane.

The end of the driveway was marked by an old mailbox shaped like Ned Kelly's helmet. Some joker had put a few bullets through it, probably so they could say they'd shot him. I pulled up on the gravel next to it and let the engine idle. The gate was wide open and I could tell from the grass growing through the bottom rung that it hadn't been closed for some time. Yet another security issue I'd have to mention to Freddy. I cracked my knuckles in preparation for a chat.

Dust rose in my wake as I drove up the driveway. A dilapidated farmhouse came into view over the rise a hundred metres farther along, the building dwarfed by a huge shed in the yard. A metal chimney protruded from its roof. Straight-away, I could smell the distinctive bittersweet ammonia odour of a cook in progress. I gagged and had to pinch my nose. I sounded the horn to make sure nobody panicked at the sight of a strange car coming up to the property.

As I parked, three men emerged from the main house.

One skinny bloke was dressed in ripped jeans and a dirty singlet. He held a pump-action shottie, its barrel pointed to the sky. The second man was much fatter and resembled a retired bikie. He was wearing leathers and sporting a long, bushy white beard, despite being bald on top. A pit bull strained at the leash he'd wrapped around his wrist, slobber dripping from its snarling jaws, eyes bulging.

These two walking clichés moved aside as their boss came out. He wore a leather vest over his stringy torso and his mottled skin was covered in faded tattoos. His hair was slick, jet black like the goatee he stroked thoughtfully as he frowned at my shiny ute. I stepped out of the car and waved in a friendly fashion that I knew would freak him right the fuck out.

Freddy, to his credit, retained his composure, though he looked a lot paler than a moment before. The bloke with the shotgun lowered the barrel to the deck and swore quietly. The one with the dog turned to Freddy for guidance. Clearly they remembered my last visit.

Freddy stepped down off the verandah to meet me, offering his hand. I shook it.

'Mate, I haven't seen you in—what—must be almost a year now? Fucken lovely set of wheels. V8, yeah?'

I shook my head.

'Righto. How's Steph going, then? You and her tied the knot yet?'

'Nah. She sends her regards,' I said quietly, sniffing and pinching my septum.

'Does she? Nice girl, that one. Ah look, come on inside, away from this fucken stink. You sort of get used to it after a while and forget how bad it is. You remember the boys?'

I nodded acknowledgement. Freddy waved the two men away. The one carrying the shotgun plonked himself down in a swing chair, resting the gun across his lap. I noticed it was still casually pointed in my general direction, but that was all right. Better to be cautious in this business. The dog lunged forward and snapped at my legs. I had to take a step back. Freddy was furious, spittle foaming at the corner of his lips.

'Bring that fucken mutt to heel, Johnno, for fuck sake.'

'Sorry, Freddy,' the heavy man mumbled, dragging the pit bull away. He tied it up to the Hill's Hoist that rotated slowly in the slight breeze. Half a dozen small T-shirts hung stiffly on the line. Freddy had two boys. I'd hoped they would be away, in school maybe. Then I remembered it was summer holidays.

As we entered the house Freddy adopted a more serious air. I had my shirt open at the neck, for effect, and he was staring.

'How's the burns, mate? Still giving you gyp?'

'They'd be fine if everyone didn't feel compelled to point them out to me all the time.'

'Oh yeah, sorry, sorry about that. It's just, well...'

An awkward moment passed while I waited for Freddy to do or say something. Blokes like him are all the same. All you have to do is stand there and glare at them, no talk, no questions. Eventually they'll spill their guts of their own accord.

Freddy's eyes were darting all over the shop as his tiny brain tried to work an angle that could get him out of the shit. 'Come out the back, meet the missus and kids,' he proposed, all pally.

'Lead on.'

The back of the house opened onto a surprisingly clean swimming pool. The two boys frolicked in the water, splashing each other and doing laps. They were both wearing plastic clothes pegs on their noses. Their tanned, rake-thin mother lay poolside on a white plastic lounger. She was wearing blue bikini bottoms and a pair of Dolce & Gabbana dinner-plate sunglasses, undoubtedly fake. She peered at us over her sunnies, pulling them down her sharp nose with a bony forefinger. Her features were pinched, ribcage visible, small breasts wrinkled before their time.

'Put your titties away, Ange. We've a visitor, for fuck sake.'

She scrabbled to snatch up her bikini top, fastening it quickly around her chest. She smiled weakly and I saw then she was pretty far gone down the glass highway. She looked like an extra from a Romero film.

'I'll get the tea on,' she said, coughing and gathering up her stuff. 'Keep an eye on the boys, Freddy. Watch they don't drown each other.'

Freddy nodded grimly. 'Yeah. Bring some biscuits out too, Ange. The good ones, not them cheap Tim Tam knockoffs.' He gestured to a white plastic chair that matched the lounger. I took a seat, stretching my legs out and squinting against the sun. Freddy sat down on the other side of the flimsy table. We watched his kids splash around for a bit before I noticed a life-size Thomas the Tank Engine smiling creepily at me from the paddock behind the pool. Its paint was faded and peeling, and it was listing at an odd angle. I craned my neck for a better look. There was a ten-foot-tall plastic T. rex on its side in the dirt next to it.

'Where'd you get those?'

'Ah, the kids wanted them. Flood-damaged bits of some old theme park down in Victoria. Paid a hundred bucks each for them.'

'A bargain.'

'So, how's business? Must be good if you're driving around in a beast like that.'

'I was going to ask you the same thing, Freddy.'

He scrunched up his face and spoke slowly. 'What do ya mean? I work for you, Ben. You're the king round here. The glass is all yours.'

'All of it?'

'Of course, yeah.'

I nodded and stretched out a crick in my neck. 'Right. It is all mine, isn't it?'

He was about to respond but I stopped him by wagging my finger. 'I pay you to manufacture the product and I deal with distribution. This is a production facility. No crystal is actually sold from here because, well, it's not yours to sell, is it? Maybe the odd Adidas employee flogs a pair of sneakers out the back of the factory now and then, but the worst that can happen to them if they get caught is they lose their job. You know how the Taliban punished thieves in Afghanistan? This is before we arrived to civilise the place, of course. Amputation of the hands. Barbaric. You can see where they're coming from, though. An effective deterrent.'

'Now hold on a minute, Ben, I didn't know who he was. He rocked up here looking to buy seven grand's worth of ice and said he was working for you...'

'So he used my name. It didn't occur to you to call me and verify that?'

'Well, no. I mean, I probably should have but he seemed legit and he said it was your money, not his. I figured you was busy and just sent someone for a re-up.'

'It was my money, Freddy. He stole it from me.'

'I didn't know that, mate—how could I?'

'And how did he know to come here? You got an ad in the local paper? Flyers with your number on 'em stuck to lampposts in Nowra?'

'I don't know. I thought you sent him, for fuck sake.'

Ange padded back out through the screen door, carrying a tray with two steaming mugs of tea and a plate of chocolate biscuits. She beat a hasty retreat. I picked up one of the biscuits, dunked it in my tea and began sucking the chocolate off it.

'Not bad. But unless these are the fanciest fucken biscuits money can buy, I believe you owe me seven large, Freddy.'

'Sure, sure. I've got it for you. Well, not all of it, but I'll have it for you in a day or two.'

I laughed quietly and shook my head, popping the rest of the biscuit in my mouth and swallowing.

'Now that I think about it, you actually owe me fourteen thou, since you gave away seven grand's worth of my glass.'

'Yeah. Suppose that's right enough. I can't really get that back for you, though.'

'I know Freddy, I know.' I took another biscuit and dipped it in the tea. 'These are pretty fancy. Ange has good taste in bickies.' I waved to his kids as I sipped the tea. Earl Grey, it was. Really hit the spot. 'That's why I'll be content to take the seven grand in cash and the other seven out of your useless fucken hide.'

I set the mug down on the tray and rose to walk to the edge of the pool. I crouched down by the water and the kids swam over to me.

'Listen, you boys better go inside and dry off. That's enough swimming for now.'

The lads exchanged a puzzled look, then to his credit the older one said, 'Fuck off, mister, you're not my da.' That tickled me, it really did.

'Ah well, have it your way. Don't say I didn't warn you.'

Freddy was out of his chair by then, unsure whether he should run or stand his ground. He probably didn't really believe I'd give him a hiding right there in front of his kids. He was frantically trying to work out how much physical damage equated to seven thousand bucks, and if he could afford it. He tried to fight me off and backed into the plastic table and chairs, sending them flying. One of the chairs skittered away and slid into the pool. The kids were frozen in the water, their mouths hanging open in shock. Thomas the Tank Engine looked on impassively, stupid grin still plastered across his face as he watched me slap the not-so-Fat Controller around.

Ange came running just as I was administering some blows to Freddy's kidneys. She was squealing for me to let him go and for a second I thought I was going to have to whack her one too, which I really didn't want to do. I have principles. Fortunately the two blokes in Freddy's crew also made an appearance. The big one threw his hands up in the air and turned away, shaking his head. The other bloke in the singlet had his shottie at the ready. Fair play to him, he met my eye as I angled Freddy's body between us just in case, his neck in the crook of my arm. He surprised me then by making a real smart move. Ange was making a beeline for me, her thongs flapping against the concrete, painted fingernails at the ready. Casual as you like the young bloke stepped up sharply and grabbed her by the arm. She cursed him and tried to break free so he flung her onto the grass and turned the shotgun on her.

'Stay there, Ange,' he said coolly, 'the boss is in a meeting.'

Shit, I was so impressed I let Freddy go after only a thousand bucks' worth of a hiding. He couldn't take much more than that anyway. He sprawled forward and almost fell in the pool, collapsing in an unruly heap by the water's edge. I nodded to the bloke with the shotgun and he lowered it, allowing Ange to crawl to her husband.

'Remind me of your name,' I said to the young guy.

'It's Patrick. Patrick Gray, from Nowra.'

'Your friends call you Paddy?'

'Not within earshot, if they know what's good for them.'

How could I not like him? If I hadn't needed someone I could at least half trust there on the farm keeping an eye on things, I would've had him running the Target Ball stand that very night. I flipped Freddy over with the toe of my boot and crouched down beside him.

'You have two days to get that seven grand, Freddy McNamara, otherwise Patrick Gray here's going to take your hands off with a hacksaw. And once you do get it, you're to give it directly to him.' I looked up at my latest recruit. 'You keep that money, Patrick. That's your retainer, and there'll be more where that came from. Call me if you think anything here's not running as smoothly as it should be.'

'Yes, Mr Wallace.'

The plastic chair clattered out of the pool behind me. Freddy's two sons climbed out after it, pulling up their sodden swim trunks, all thin, gangly limbs, flattened hair and scared eyes. It was a scorcher of a day, but they were both shivering.

7

It's easy to go insane working at the Kingdom without something else to do. Steph and I were so desperate for a distraction from the daily grind that we even paid Cactus World in Gilgandra a visit. The fucken place was closed for a holiday, so we had to settle for a glimpse of some bloke's extensive collection of cacti through a wire fence. It was devastating, in a funny sort of way. Clearly we needed to get out more.

'How many of the "big" things have you seen?' Steph asked me as we climbed reluctantly back into the ute.

'Not that many,' I told her, thinking about it. 'The Big Worm, the Big Yabby and the Big Merino are the only ones I remember.'

'Oh yeah, that big sheep's a popular one.'

'You must have seen loads.' Steph had travelled right around Australia when she was younger and even more of a hippie.

'Um, let's see. I've been to the Big Ant, the Big Diplodocus, the Big Pavlova, the Big Prawn of course, the Big Dugong, the Big Scotsman and a couple of others.'

'How many of these cultural icons are there, anyway?'

'About a hundred and fifty, I think. Be funny to see them all.'

'The road trip of a fucken lifetime.' I consulted the clock on the dashboard. It was almost eleven. The show wouldn't be open for another couple of hours. 'I could go a big pie,' I told Steph, who groaned and agreed that it was probably time for second breakfast.

We drove to one of the town pubs and parked right outside. The street was mostly empty. The heat was enough to put off any pedestrians. Old men at the bar looked up from their pots of beer as we entered. Other than a few obligatory double takes at my neck, no one paid us much attention. The old men resumed contemplation of their beers as Steph and I slid into a booth.

The place had been fitted out to resemble an Irish pub, with snugs lining one wall allowing small groups to drink in relative privacy. A flat-screen television dominated the main wall, showing an old rugby match. Apart from the quartet of old farts propping up the bar, the only other patron was a bloke in his twenties staring into his drink in the booth behind ours.

'You know, I don't usually do it, but I gave myself a card reading last night.'

'Yeah? What'd you find out? Tall dark stranger on the horizon?'

'No. I hope you're not going to make fun of this. It's serious.'

'Is it? You better go ahead and tell me, then.'

'It's pretty much what I suspected anyway. The Four of Swords came out, as did the High Priestess. Those are both pretty appropriate, given our situation.'

'Your situation, you mean.'

'Yeah, right, exactly. So the Four of Swords is an eye-of-the-hurricane card. That means an ordeal has ended and for the moment I will have a period of quiet, some time to reflect before potential danger returns.'

'I don't get it. How does that apply?'

'Well, we got my car back and I'm helping you expand the business. Two ticks there. And as for the High Priestess— well, I'm going to interpret that as a sign of the Shadow, the whispering inner voice that is about to emerge in order to transform my personality into something more powerful.'

'Righto. What do you think: steak and bacon pie, or steak and mushroom? Anything about that in there?'

I don't think she even heard me. She was on one of her rolls.

'Add to that the Eight of Cups, which generally indicates the need to move on emotionally, and the Page of Pentacles, which almost never comes out in a reading, and it's pretty clear what my immediate future holds. The Page of Pentacles is a wealth card, more precisely suggesting that I will soon have the opportunity to manage a lot of money.'

'I like that one. What's this about moving on emotionally, though? Am I getting the boot here?'

She snapped out of her train of thought and stared at me as if she'd forgotten I was there.

'God no. Don't worry, babe, you're safe. What I think that means is that all the other men I've known are going to start fading from my memory.'

I snorted. 'You think about these blokes often, do you?'

'The thing is, I only spent time with them because part of me knew that they were just temporary. What I remember about them should start to fragment now, to fall apart and crumble.'

I'd seen that faraway expression on her face a thousand times. It was time for me to tune out.

'I'll forget their foxy scent, their sharp stubble against my neck, their calloused hands, the way they frowned or rolled their eyes when I explained how I make a living. They'll be like jigsaw pieces being put back in the box. Their faces will melt into one distinct male form, their chests and backs and legs and dicks will all shrink or expand to become one standard-size chunk of masculinity. I'll forget the details— the scars, the tattoos, the kinks, the annoying laughs, the bad breath and petty obsessions. I'll struggle to recall their accents, the size of their feet, the colour of their eyes. All traces of their individuality will be slowly erased until all that remains is a single man, my Benji. His burns, his muscly forearms, his cynicism, his loaded silences, all folded into a concrete force as powerful and real as the pleasure he brings me every night. He is wondrous, this man, a marvel, a thing of great beauty, and he is all mine.'

'He's right here, you know.'

She climbed down from her flying unicorn then and waved a hand under her chin. She was close to tears. Sometimes, she almost scares me with this shit.

'God. Sorry, was that a bit much?'

'Just a tad. That was some reading.'

'Incredible. I know.'

She calmed down and studied the menu. I considered reminding her of what she said about people reading what they want to hear into the cards, but thought better of it. I should have known it was all leading somewhere. She closed the menu and hit me with her latest proposal.

'You know that course I've been wanting to do in Melbourne?'

'Remind me.'

'The kinesiology one, at the College of Natural Medicine.'

'Which is what again?'

She tutted. 'It's diagnosing long-term physical problems by assessing if the chakras are out of balance. It's amazing stuff. You remember that neck pain I was having? A kinesiologist told me it was because of unresolved issues with my mum. She was so on the money.'

I rolled my eyes. 'Sounds scientific.'

'Don't be so cynical all the time. You should try it. Honestly, it might help you with your issues.'

'You know what would help me with my issues? A cold beer. What do you want to order?'

At the bar I opted for the steak and bacon pie with chips. Steph wanted a salad. She was on yet another weird diet. This time she had convinced herself she was allergic to gluten. Last month it was dairy. I supposed next month it would be oxygen. Didn't stop her having a glass of Sauv Blanc, I noticed. As I paid the haggard-looking barmaid, the door to the pub swung open to admit a gaunt young fella wearing a baseball cap that was way too big for his pinhead.

I watched him in the mirror behind the bar. He stood by the door for a minute, scanning the room to see who was there, then proceeded to the booth where the other young bloke was sitting. He tugged at the crotch of his loose jeans as he sat opposite, nodding a cursory greeting and pulling the rim of his hat down over his eyes. Fucken ridiculous. He might as well have been wearing a badge that said DEALER.

I carried the glasses back to our booth. The young bloke who'd just arrived looked me up and down as I neared, but I blanked him and sat just out of sight. He was right behind us, which suited me fine.

'The only thing about this course in Melbourne is that it's pretty exy,' Steph said as she sipped her wine.

'How much we talking?'

'Eight thousand.'

I waved my hand. 'Don't worry about it. Book yourself in and I'll shout you.'

'Really? Just like that?'

'Whatever makes you happy.' I was about to ask her how much time she'd need off from the Kingdom when she abruptly raised a finger to shush me. The blokes in the booth behind were deep in conversation and some detail had caught her attention. I sipped my beer and listened.

'Look, I could only get seventy-five.'

'I told you it was a fucken hundred.'

'That's all I have. Sorry.'

'Fuck. You're such a little bitch, homes. You know this is good glass, right? You gets what you pays for.'

'Sorry, Matt. I'll have the rest by Saturday, promise.'

'You fucken better. Here. Now buy me a pot, ya cunt.'

We drank in silence as the first guy went to the bar. I tapped my fingers on the table and raised my eyebrows at Steph.

'Does he work for you?' she whispered.

I shook my head. 'Not that I know of. Not yet, anyway.'

'We should follow them.'

'You're getting into this, eh?'

'You got something else on this arvo?'

'True. And I did just spend eight grand on knievelology, so...'

'*Kinesiology.* Jeez, you're such a dickhead.'

'A dickhead with deep pockets.' I leaned across the table and spoke quietly. 'You want to see how this works? We'll go after him when he leaves, see where he's holed up. Probably just a backyard lab, but still. Worth a look.'

Our lunch came, and the dealer seemed content to continue humiliating his client for a while with barbs about his uselessness. He was just asking for someone to step in and take over his business. I'd come across a hundred like him, small-time entrepreneurs who thought that just because they could cook a decent batch they were Walter fucken White. The two blokes left together and I had to gather up the remaining half of my pie in a napkin. Steph shoved a few of my chips in her mouth as we got up to leave.

As we emerged into the harsh sunlight, a filthy old Toyota was pulling away from the kerb, smoke pluming from its exhaust. The recipient of the deal was walking away down the street in the opposite direction. I didn't care about him— the dealer was my focus. We climbed casually into the ute.

'Keep your distance,' Steph told me as I struggled to eat the remains of the pie while steering.

'I know how to follow someone.'

'You're getting crumbs on everything.'

'It's my car.'

'He's turning left.'

'Since he's driving the only car on the road other than ours, I noticed that, yes, thank you.'

'Where do you think he's going?'

I sighed as I made the turn. 'Crank World, maybe. Or the Big Meth Pipe. How the fuck would I know? Home, probably.'

The Toyota limped into a dead-end street, smoke still belching from its rear. There were two dilapidated weatherboard houses on either side of the road and he pulled into the driveway of the one at the end on the left. I slowed down for a second to get a look, then drove on. I turned back towards the main street and pulled in to park out of the line of sight of the house, killing the engine.

I was out of the car in a flash, crouching at the rear wheel to watch the dealer unlock the front door of his house and disappear inside. My hands instinctively clutched for the ghost rifle and I shook my fingers out in irritation. I couldn't seem to stop that tic.

Filthy, tattered curtains hung in the windows of the house, and they were pulled shut. The lawn was baked yellow in the few spots where it had somehow managed to survive—the front was a dustbowl. The building had been painted sky blue at some point but most of the colour was gone now, the paint faded and peeling in the sun. The stumps had sunk on one side, giving the house a distinct lean. Home sweet fucken home.

I spent a few more minutes watching for further movements but saw nothing. I made a note of the street name and climbed back into the driver's seat. Steph had been watching the house in the rear-view mirror.

'What do you think? Are we going to pay him a visit?'

'Oh, it's "we" now, is it? You're game all of a sudden.'

'You've got one of those metal rod thingos you use to change tyres. I could hit him with that.'

'A tyre iron. Well, you could, but it's probably not advisable. Baby steps. We'll come back tonight and have a poke around if he's not home.'

'This is not as much fun as I expected.'

'You'll get your chance.'

The crowds were beginning to form by the time we got back to the Kingdom. Despite the baking afternoon heat, over-enthusiastic kids had managed to persuade their parents to drag them around the carnival, looking forward to plastering fairy floss all over their faces and going home with overpriced show bags filled with crap. Steph and I watched a dozen different family units struggling to extricate strollers from the boots of cars while trying not to lose their temper at impatient toddlers.

'Still keen on popping out a couple of sprogs?' I asked Steph as we trundled slowly through the car park towards the staff parking area.

'Gives you pause, doesn't it? Look at those angry, sweaty faces. Some of these couples are probably five years younger than us and they look ten years older.' She turned back to me and placed a hand on my thigh. 'I don't want us to end up like that, Ben. We'll do things different, eh?'

'My oath we will.'

'I never imagined myself having a child until I met you. Now I can't imagine anything else. I always dreamed of saving enough money telling fortunes and giving massages to be able to open a little kinesiology and yoga studio on the Gold Coast. I could rent out the space for life drawing and Pilates classes, teach Ayurvedic massage and align the chakras of people who need my help, go home at night to a man who is glad to see me, maybe a couple of kids who'll show me the drawings they've done at school. I could stick them to the refrigerator using magnets shaped like dinosaurs and ask them if they want Vegemite or Promite in tomorrow's sandwiches. We could share baths and maybe fool around a little until the kids burst in and we have to disguise what we're doing under the bubbles.'

Running the aircon all the time made my eyes dry up so I switched it off and cracked the window. It was like a furnace out there. Why these parents didn't just wait until evening was beyond me. I guess they thought being out at the show with their screaming offspring was a better option than being stuck in the house with them. Steph was right about that much. No way we were going down that road, no way. I'd be hiring a fucken nanny to do all that shit for me. And if the kids wanted to play, well, we'd just step off the front deck onto the beach. You won't see me being dragged around Big Dubs on a Sunday afternoon. I'll be kicking back in a hammock, beer in my hand, watching the kids splash in the surf while I mentally count my money. A house on the Gold Coast, a couple of dirt bikes in the garage and a big fuck-off four-wheel-drive parked outside? Fucken perfect. If Steph was up for playing the dutiful wife and mother, well, maybe it was worth the hassle. I could pretend to be a good family man, sit on the local council or some shit. No one would suspect a fucken thing.

'I don't think it's unrealistic, this dream.' She wasn't talking to me anymore now. 'It's not out of reach like the ones I hear from all those women who seek me out on the Kingdom. This one is possible, and best of all it's up to us. We'll have a son one day, you and me. You wait and see. His little neck will smell like my pop's hair pomade, and he'll squeeze me tighter than anyone ever has.'

A hot wind blew in through the window. I closed my eyes and winced. We were locked in a queue of traffic, waiting to get through the entrance. With the feel of warm air on my neck and Steph's soft voice imagining some chakra-aligned future we might or might not have, I began to drift.

I was in the back of a truck rolling down some desert road. The heat was heavy and suffocating, pressing down on my torso. A burning sensation pulsed in my chest, making me think the dressing needed changing. I sat up painfully, groggy from the heat and medication. I carefully peeled back the edge of the bandage to peer underneath. The wounds were still raw and inflamed, still made my stomach churn. I stuck the dressing down and leaned my temple against the cool metal frame of the truck, feeling the vibrations of the engine drilling into my skull.

Another man lay on a stretcher opposite me. He was absorbed in reading something on his Kindle, seemingly oblivious to the fact his right leg was missing below the knee. Woozily, I shuffled along the bench to the rear, where a soldier in combat gear sat quietly smoking as he looked out at the Humvee travelling behind us, just visible in the darkness. His M4 lay unsecured across his lap, bouncing with the movement of the vehicle like it might fall out onto the dusty road at any minute. Without speaking, he offered me a cigarette. I desperately wanted one but I had to refuse. Doctor's orders.

I stared out at the black desert, glad for a cool breeze on my skin. The sky lit up briefly in the distance, off to the east. The sound of a faraway explosion reached our ears a moment later, a low rumbling echo, comforting in its familiarity. Several more bright streaks punctured the horizon: Hydra rockets released from the belly of an Apache gunship. They vanished into the darkness only to be replaced a second later by a starburst of fire as they found their target. Another enemy destroyed, or maybe one of our own. We could never be certain.

'Ben. Ben, are you even listening?'

Steph clicked her fingers. I snapped back and nodded.

'Yeah, yeah. The Gold Coast. Something about dinosaurs.'

Irritated, she pointed to the gap that had opened up between us and the car in front. I slipped the gearstick into drive and we rolled forward another twenty metres. In the distance the engine brakes of an eighteen-wheeler moaned from the highway, a great monster taking a breath.

8

Two of the six streetlamps in the row were out, creating a shadowy umbrella at the end of the road. I leaned against one that wasn't fizzing as it strained to blink back into life. Even with decent lighting, I would have been difficult to spot. I was wearing dark clothes and standing perfectly still. This was the sort of sentry duty I was used to, quietly watching and waiting for signs of movement.

My ears became attuned to the background noise and I could hear various animals in the distance. Two cats were standing off somewhere in the neighbourhood, a territorial struggle punctuated by low growls and banshee-like screaming as they went at each other. A dog barked, his rough howl curtailed by a sharp word from his master. Above me, a family of possums walked the tightrope of telephone lines from one side of the street to the other.

The screen of my phone lit up. I cupped my hand to hide the glare and read Steph's text message.

Coast is clear. Looks lk pizza and xbox on menu. Glad I brought a magazine.

I quickly typed a reply.

Let me know when he's OM.

I was about to put the phone away when it flashed again.

???

Oscar Mike.

And that is?

On the move, ffs.

Yessir, general.

I was a corporal.

Is that higher or lower?

Stop txting now. I'm going in.

Righto. Maintaining radio silence as of now. X

Knocking on a meth dealer's front door and politely informing him I would be his boss from that point on was hardly an option, unless I fancied picking a shiv out from between my ribs. I wanted to have a good look around in there first, see what sort of set-up he had, decide if it was even worth my while muscling in on his piss-ant operation.

Satisfied no one was home, I slipped the phone into my pocket and walked quickly across the road, careful to avoid the pools of light under the streetlamps.

No one saw me as I approached the house. Gilgandra was asleep.

After the Kingdom had closed for the night, it hadn't taken much to persuade Steph to come on the surveillance detail. She was in with both feet now. A ruthless streak was emerging in her. It would be interesting to see how far she was prepared to go.

Matt had emerged from the house only a few minutes after we'd pulled up around the corner. I'd been prepared for an all-night vigil but he'd jumped in his crappy Toyota and taken off. We were in Steph's Datsun, low-key enough for a surveillance op. She followed him at a sensible distance with the headlights switched off while I became a sentinel.

I tracked along the side of the house, navigating through piles of garbage bags and boxes. I paused to examine the rubbish. Dozens of empty Codral packets had been crushed and piled into a larger cardboard box. Amateur cooks often extracted pseudoephedrine from cold and flu tablets, though why they would leave such an obvious marker out in the open for any fucker to find was beyond me. They might as well have put a sign up on the front lawn inviting the AFP in for a snort.

The back of the house gave out onto a long yard overgrown with native plants. A battered old couch sat in the middle, covered in overflowing ashtrays. A meth pipe lay on its side on a rickety wooden table, next to a copy of *Zoo Weekly*.

I picked up the pipe and sniffed. The sharp odour almost

made me gag. This was rough stuff they were smoking. There was a pitiful-looking lemon tree in one corner of the yard but it did nothing to mask the stench emanating from the house. I covered my nose and mouth as I approached the back door.

My intention had been to smash the glass with my elbow so I could reach in and undo the latch but the fucken door was unlocked. Asking for it, they were. Just waiting for someone like me to roll up and set them straight.

All of the lights in the house were off and after only a couple of steps I kicked something that skittered across the kitchen tiles. I stopped and took my phone out again so I could use the display as a weak torch. The kitchen was a predictable mess of empty bottles, cans and take-away containers, most of which still had food welded to their insides. The sink was piled high with dishes. Blowies buzzed over plates and pots, revelling in such fertile breeding grounds. It was disgusting.

I followed my nose to the bathroom, along a carpeted hallway. I pushed the door open gently and shone the phone inside, still reluctant to switch on any lights. The bathroom had been set up as a primitive lab and the smell was so strong that my first instinct was to crack open the window. If Matt or some other skinny prick were cooking up in such a confined space, it would only be a matter of time before they dropped dead from inhaling such toxic fumes. How they had survived this long was a miracle.

The house would surely have to be condemned after they cleared out or expired. No one would want to buy it. You can never get rid of that smell. Best thing to do would be to put a match to the place and stand well back. That's what happened with most amateur labs in the end, anyway. A little carelessness or inexperience mixing chemicals and boom—obliterated, like someone had called in a targeted drone strike.

Carefully closing the door behind me, I continued to search the house. The lounge room at the end of the hallway wasn't in as bad a state as I expected. Matt probably conducted a lot of his deals there and that required some semblance of order. A large flat-screen television had been attached to one wall. I didn't recognise the brand—it was probably one of those cheap knockoffs they sell at JB. Half a dozen game controllers littered the coffee table. It could easily have passed for any unkempt share-house lounge room, if not for the omnipresent stench of meth.

I'd passed two bedroom doors en route to the lounge and I retraced my steps to check them out. The first was larger and had clothes strewn haphazardly across the floor. The bed was unkempt and filthy-looking. I relaxed. This really was just another small-time meth operation, one of a thousand the cops would never know about. Nobody was going to leap from a cupboard, Uzi blazing.

The second bedroom was smaller and had obviously been intended for a child. A narrow single mattress lay on the floor and a few meagre possessions were arranged on the carpet next to it. It was the bunk of someone passing through, a transient tweaker recruited to assist with the cook in exchange for free glass.

I was about to close the door behind me when I spotted a faded Fremantle Dockers guernsey draped over the back of a chair. I angled my phone towards it.

It was the same kind as the one Mikey had worn when he worked on the Kingdom. I lifted it to my face and inhaled the owner's sweat but I couldn't tell if it was Mikey or not. It was possible that he was here, yet it didn't seem likely. The Dockers had a lot of fans in the east. And surely Mikey would have spent some of his stolen loot on a new shirt.

I scanned the room for any other telltale signs. Anyone could have been staying there, any dumb crank addict headed nowhere.

I threw the shirt down and started kicking things. I put my boot through a cupboard door and it got stuck for a moment before I wrenched it out. I flipped the mattress over and ripped the curtains down.

There wasn't enough for me to wreck, so I went back into the larger bedroom and pulled all the drawers out of the dresser, upending their contents onto the already considerable pile of unwashed clothes. It was already so messy in there it would take the owner a couple of minutes to realise the place had been done over. Not that he was going to have that luxury, as I'd be up in his grill the minute he crossed the fucken threshold.

The fourth drawer was heavier than the rest. I flipped it over and a knot of underwear fell out, none of it particularly fresh. A plastic baggie of cash was taped to the underside. I tore it loose and tossed the drawer away. It looked like a lot of money but it was mostly fives, tens and twenties, no pineapples. The typical roll of a meth dealer. At a glance, it looked to be around a thousand bucks. Whoop-de-fuck-en-doo. Still, always good to have some small change for Target Ball.

There had to be a stash of meth somewhere in the house. I stalked out into the corridor to search for it when my phone began buzzing insistently. I answered it as I started my sweep of the lounge room.

'Can you talk?'

'Yeah. What is it?'

'Elvis has left the building. Must have been just making a drop. Maybe having a quick bump. He's heading back now with a friend.'

'Good. I'd like to have a word with him.'

'Listen, there was a bit of a ruckus over here. Raised voices.'

'Arguing over fucken Mario Kart, were they?'

'Boys will be boys. That's probably it. Anyway, there's two of them now so be careful.'

'I'll handle it.'

'I'm in hot pursuit of the target now. Hey, I quite like all this skulking around. This is the best date we've been on in ages.'

'Better than Cirque du Soleil? Those tickets were fucken expensive.'

'Oh yeah, that was pretty good.'

'So when you get here, wait outside till I call you in, just to be on the safe side.'

'Aww, but I brought my rounders bat with the barbed wire wrapped around it.'

'You've still got that?'

'Sometimes a guy comes in for a massage with the wrong idea.'

'That would persuade him otherwise. But no sense in you being a witness to anything that might damage your delicate sensibility.'

'My sensibility's not as delicate as it used to be.'

'I'm starting to get that, yeah. Look, I better get in position. They'll be here in a couple of minutes.'

'Righto. Save some for me, though.'

I dragged a cheap hard-backed chair to the far corner, facing the door. Next to it I placed a lamp, one of those silver Ikea ones with a flexible neck. I plugged it into the wall socket and tested it. I turned the shade downwards to the floor, so I would only be dimly lit when it came on. Satisfied I would not be noticed when they first came in the door, I removed the nine mil from the back of my pants and took a seat, crossing my legs and setting the gun on my thigh.

It was deathly quiet in the house and as I waited in the darkness I thought about walking in the desert at night. The hospital where I'd spent six weeks recuperating had been far from the action. During those early days the worst thing was seeing people's reactions to my burns. Even the staff couldn't help but wince sometimes. I spent a lot of time wandering, trying to regain fitness, though the doctors said I couldn't run in case the sores opened.

I would walk out past the perimeter of the hospital grounds, past the point where the grass met the sand. I wasn't supposed to be out there but it wasn't like on the operating posts. There were no anti-personnel mines buried in the dirt, no IEDs waiting to tear you to shreds. Nothing much at all, really.

After sunset was the time to go. The burning sensation in my chest would ease in the cold until it almost vanished completely. I realised then that I'd spend the rest of my life in the shadows. No more sunbaking on the beach, no kicking a footy around the park, no more long lunches out the front of cafés. I had to become something else. Something new.

The Toyota chugged into the driveway. Its exhaust backfired with a gunshot crack and I knew that every animal within a five-mile radius had just raised their head at the sound and sniffed the air for danger.

VOLTAN, MASTER OF ELECTRICITY

For most of this past year I have had trouble remembering. At first I presumed this was an inevitable result of ageing, but then it was delicately pointed out to me that I'm not terribly old—fifty-eight, which may seem ancient to some, but is still within the boundaries of middle age, technically speaking. Put it this way: if I dropped dead tomorrow, those who knew me would surely opine, 'Oh, but he was still so *young.*' At least I hope they would. In any event, fifty-eight hardly seems old enough to warrant the desolate field that now occupies the place where my memory used to be.

Under duress, I went to see someone about it a few months ago, during the Kingdom's winter break. I joked throughout the tiresome questioning about early onset Alzheimer's and the physician played along until it got to the part about my history with electric current. I was frank with my interlocutor and he repaid my honesty in kind. It turns out that the repeated application of dangerously high voltage to my cranium may have affected my episodic memory, in that it would appear to be in the process of erasing itself.

Perhaps I should have paid more heed to what I assumed at the time was mere alarmist chatter about possible long-term brain damage. My detractors have been proven correct, after a fashion. My semantic memory is relatively undamaged: I can recall facts, skills, languages, indeed many nuggets of useless information I've managed to acquire down the years. What's largely absent is my memory of events—where I went, and what I did there. Some hazy recollections remain, sparked by a strong memory of a person who was present at the time, but these are sadly few and far between.

It's a frustrating condition, but in a perverse way I have also found it to be liberating. We passed through Mount Gambier this year and although I know the Kingdom was there roughly a decade ago, I had no memory of the visit. Consequently the streets were new to me, as if I were seeing them for the first time. Staring into the azure waters that fill the huge volcanic crater overlooking the town was quite a thrill. I had been there before—I must have been, as I would not have passed up the chance to view such a natural wonder—but nothing of that day a decade hence remained.

It irritates no end those who would call me friend. Their allegiance to the minor events of the past has always puzzled me, however. Now at least I have an excuse when I fail to recall the afternoon we all played mini-golf in Colac after the radiator overheated on the truck hauling the Ferris wheel. The others each have their own distinct memories of the day, often so vivid they can even list what I was wearing (purple culottes, allegedly, and a red-and-white-striped cape that I honestly do not recall owning). The truth of the matter, which I would never speak aloud lest it cause offence, is that the day was likely of such little significance to me that I wouldn't even have remembered it before my memory began to crumble.

The doctor told me that I will continue to form new episodic memories, but they too will vanish within a few years until, eventually, I won't be able to remember what I did or where I went a fortnight ago. I will be forever trapped in the present—the ultimate Buddhist, if you will. Perhaps my life will become an inspiration for those who wish to forget.

My physician also suggested I document what memories remain clear now, before they are whisked away. He claimed this would be a useful and enjoyable exercise, but that I should not expect reading them in the future to trigger any emotional response. Once my memories are wiped, they will be gone forever. When I read over my notes in later life, what I have written will be unknown to me. I will believe it to be pure fiction. Yet I wonder—isn't it the same for everyone? Don't we reinvent who we were all the time? Aren't our memories little more than a series of misremembered anecdotes, exaggerations and wishful thinking? Perhaps I shall not be so very different to anyone else.

Preservation of the past has been one of humankind's chief preoccupations for centuries, although I am not convinced much of it is worth preserving. As for my own stories: when I sit down in my trailer with a pen and paper to record them before they are forgotten, my feeling toward much of what has happened to me in life is one of ambivalence. I am haunted by the inescapable truth that little of what I have done has mattered to anyone. To the casual outsider my existence as a sideshow act on a travelling carnival may seem the antithesis of boring—but upon reflection, I see I have had an unremarkable life. Much of it is not even worth recording. Who would I be recording it for? Myself, in dotage, bored by the past of a man I fail to recognise? I prefer to let most of it fade away. In some cases, it is perhaps preferable to forget.

Please don't mistake my cynicism for regret. There have been moments worthy of the annals, of that there can be no doubt. They are simply tricky to recall. Tragedy touched my life, of course, but also comedy, and love, and friendship. What did Robert Louis Stevenson say? 'Of what shall a man be proud, if he is not proud of his friends?' Now that is a sentiment I would firmly echo.

All that remains to me now are my friends—my family on the Kingdom. They are not phantoms but real, physical beings, a constant reminder of who I am, and sometimes of who I used to be. This is why it pleased me so that a man I have known since he was only a slip of a lad, a man, in fact, whose very birth I witnessed, sought me out for advice. He is a walking repository of my memories, carrying them within him now that I am unable to do so myself. When I see him, I remember.

Benjamin paid me a visit shortly after that young raga-muffin recruit of his had absconded with a considerable sum of his funds, not to mention his lady friend's motorcar. It had been some time since he had darkened my door. In fact the date of his last visit eludes me, like so much else. I did not harbour any ill will on this account. Evidently, his nose had been pressed firmly to the grindstone.

'Alakazam, stranger.'

'Alakazam, Huw.' He was the only person whom I tolerated using my real name. 'What you fiddling with there?'

I turned the object over and held it up to the light.

'This is a medium-voltage expulsion fuse with an element fashioned from copper. Normally filled with boric acid, this one was unfortunately spent earlier this year whilst testing some equipment, causing some rather noxious gases to be expelled from the tip. Not ideal for the person staring into it at the time.'

'I'm guessing that would be your former assistant.'

'The long-suffering Veronica. A lass of exemplary forti-tude, though she had her shortcomings. An accident was inevitable, I'm afraid.'

He sat down on the step next to me. I let him be for a few moments before broaching the subject all and sundry were chirruping about.

'I heard about your misfortune. Any news of the scoun-drel's whereabouts?'

'Not yet.'

'Someone will surely spy him out. No doubt he will be profligate with his windfall and draw attention to himself.'

'He couldn't have gone far in that old Datsun anyway. It's on its last legs.'

'As are we all. You have my sympathies, my dear boy. If you ever catch him, my electric chair is at your disposal.'

That prospect seemed to cheer him somewhat.

'The loss of an assistant can be most vexing. It hasn't been the same around here since Veronica left.'

'There were rumours you and her...'

'Don't be preposterous. I was more than thirty years her senior.'

'Still. She was easy on the eye.'

'I will concede that point, yes. I don't wish to be indiscreet, but her assets, if you will, were useful in drawing a crowd. However, there are plenty of naïve young fools out there who would make perfectly suitable replacements. You will find one too, I'm sure.'

'That's not the point. After all I did for him, that little prick betrayed my trust. I'm going to find him, and drag him back here so he understands exactly what that means.'

'You shouldn't work yourself up so, Benjamin. The turnover of hired hands around here is legendary.'

'He *stole* from me, Huw. You know the code. You practically wrote it. It's just not done.'

'If we stuck to the letter of the code, we'd still be settling our grievances with knives. Target Ball's an easy stand to recruit for. You'll find someone else. Let it pass.'

'I can't. Not this time. You don't understand.'

'It's hardly worth dwelling upon.'

'You don't run from the Kingdom, not after they've taken you in, and not with someone's property. You just don't.'

The poor, ruined boy—so filled with anger these days. I never had a son of my own, but...well, it's no secret I always had a soft spot for the lad.

The tornado in my mind subsided as the skies cleared, and suddenly there it was—a memory, crisp and fresh, so present it might well have happened only yesterday. I felt a warm buzz in my chest and reached across to pat Ben on the shoulder, by way of thanks. If I were ever to lose him, so much of me would slip away too.

'It is every boy's dream to run away and join a travelling show, but on rare occasions, it happens the other way around. I once knew such a boy.'

Ben stared off into the distance, raising a hand to stroke the scars under his chin. 'I suppose you did,' he said, quietly.

Without his presence on the step of my trailer, my past would be obscure to me, lost. But memory is reciprocal. Locked within me is Ben's childhood, those years that he has undoubtedly forgotten, either by accident or design. It is ironic, perhaps, that his physical embodiment is required as a key, that his past does not exist until he appears before me now. And yet, without a reminder of who we once were, how can we possibly understand what we have become?

*

This is the story of a boy called Benji. His mother, Evalisse, was a tattooed lady who swallowed swords and danced wearing naught but her ink. She was a striking beauty, with many suitors. His father, Francis, a malign individual, came from a long line of thespians and performers, stretching back to the glory days of vaudeville, or so he claimed. Rather than seek a career on the stage, Francis chose instead to use his limited powers of persuasion to hoodwink and embezzle unsuspecting members of the public.

I knew them both. Had I not been betrothed to my now-departed wife, may the Lord bless and keep her, I might well have counted myself amongst the retinue of Evalisse's frenetic courtiers. How the unpleasant, ill-tempered Francis Wallace came to capture her heart when so many better men had failed to do so can be chalked up as one of love's great inexplicable, not to mention frustrating, mysteries. He did nothing to deserve such a charming woman.

And yet Evalisse granted the repugnant Francis permission to enter her boudoir. Perhaps she saw some potential in him that others could not. Perhaps he was a different man in private, a caring, tender husband. Or perhaps he simply was well endowed. The matter has yet to be independently verified.

Both of these idiosyncratic individuals were already firmly ensconced in the Kingdom when I became part of her retinue in the spring of '78. I came to antipodean shores from the town of Ynyshir, in the Rhondda Valley, for the same reason any Welshman might migrate—to seek gainful employment, and for love. My heart had been won by a certain Catherine Butler, an Australian beauty with the calm tenacity and sturdy thighs of a mountaineer. I have heard it said that meeting a woman teaches one more about the world than reading Tolstoy ever will, even if, ultimately, the encounter leads to one's own destruction. This was certainly true of Cathy, whom I promptly married, providing me with a passport to the edge of the world and an unexpected new life.

Our first years in Australia were difficult. The only joy we had was in exploring nature, which Cathy loved to do. I was young then, and open to the idea of adventure. Money was tight. There was not much call for a failed electrical engineer with a penchant for the stage. But Cathy stuck by me through it all. She was my assistant as far as the public were concerned, my manager and the brains of the operation behind the scenes. We toured small towns, appearing at markets and school fêtes as I perfected my routine. If the Kingdom had not come along when it did, neither the act nor our marriage would have lasted.

But this is not our story. That tale is for another day, when I am in the mood for a more maudlin recollection. Needless to say, something of the dread atmosphere in the mining village, from the parlour of my mother's bleak cottage, followed me across the ocean. Some dark thing—a stain that could not be washed out. When my father came home from the mine he would spend hours in the bathroom, scrubbing his fingernails until his flesh was raw, while my mother washed his clothes in the sink. The water was always black.

Cathy was taken from me one day, you see, and another too, but we shall not speak of her. To say her name aloud is to plunge oneself into a terrible void. The return journey is too long, too arduous.

We are intent on exploring the origin of Benji, the son of Evalisse and Francis Wallace. I knew them both for several years before their courtship began in earnest. Evalisse and Cathy were friends. Francis and I were not. Evalisse was one of the most popular acts on the alley—no surprise, given the rampant nudity in her show. Francis made a pittance on his Target Ball stand, due, no doubt, to his sour demeanour and tendency to cheat the customers at every opportunity.

He was part of an unsavoury ring of carnies ready to fleece any suckers who unwittingly wandered down side-show alley seeking entertainment. Their technique was to rub chalk on their palms and pat the unsuspecting member of the public on the back, thus leaving a white handprint on their coat or shirt. For the duration of the marks' visit to the Kingdom, other stallholders were able to distinguish them and entice them to empty their pockets. The Kingdom, suffice to say, was no place for the gullible.

I rather resented this practice. My living was made honestly, through showmanship, and not without a hint of peril. Those who came to see my act were entertained, at least. Often alarmed, too. It was, for the most part, relatively safe, though had it not been for Cathy I would surely have gone into cardiac arrest on numerous occasions.

Benji was born in 1981, not a year after Evalisse and

Francis tied the knot. Evalisse had taken leave from dancing and sword swallowing early in the pregnancy, understandably, and this infuriated Francis. She was the main earner for the couple, so he was forced to redouble his efforts on Target Ball. I knew early on that the childhood of Benjamin Wallace would be fraught. Francis urged his mother back on stage mere months after the child was born, and clearly felt the boy's sole worth would be in replacing him on the stall as soon as he came of age—which, in the carnival world, can be as young as seven years old.

He forbade her from breastfeeding too, his perverse logic being that her milk-swollen breasts would attract more custom, but she managed to defy him in this regard. Poor Benji. Until he was a toddler, the tyke spent a lot of time alone, in his bassinet, ignored by his father and, it pains me to say it, neglected by his mother. This was not really her fault. When the Kingdom was in full swing, she performed at least twelve shows a day. Cathy and I helped out when we could but, alas, we too were attempting to earn a meagre crust in the backwaters of the country, and had our own child to raise.

And so Benji grew, and found his feet, and pottered quietly in the dust. Often the only sounds that came out of him were the engines of diggers, which he emulated as he played with his toy trucks. I don't believe I heard him utter a complete sentence until he was three or four. He had been hanging around our tent, watching the show from a shy distance. He won me over by asking if I could do magic.

I told him I could, in a way, and from that moment on we were firm friends.

It is not an easy life for carnival children. Their home is itinerant and they have a tendency to lose their innocence too young, to become sly and cynical. There were other kids to keep Benji company—older children, perhaps not the best influence. They practically raised themselves, that gang of dirty little waifs. It was all the adults could do to keep them in check, to prevent them from becoming too light-fingered or cruel. Benji was a stout fellow who learned to fight long before most children have to face such a challenge. I counselled him when I could, particularly if he bore fresh bruises.

As he sprouted it became increasingly obvious, at least to me, that he did not really belong on the Kingdom. His mind was elsewhere, his gaze always on the horizon. I knew that look all too well, having worn it myself for many years. We were misfits in a world of misfits. He was not especially close to either of his parents, despite his mother's best efforts to win him to her bosom. She had no more children, and the one she did have resented the life of hollow transience she had borne him into. It was clear he had little time for his brute of a father.

Even as a sallow youth, at age nine or ten, Benji openly avowed his intention to leave. Francis had him running the stall when he should have been enjoying the simple pleasures of boyhood, not to mention receiving an education. His schooling was rudimentary, at best. The Kingdom was always on the road. Occasionally he would endure a school term somewhere, if we were shut down for the winter, but it would not last. His friends were few, and those he did have would be left by the wayside when the show moved on. I felt sorry for the lad. He just wanted some semblance of a normal life, no doubt.

It was really only a matter of time before Benji absconded. The most heartbreaking aspect of his flight was that no one noticed he was gone for two days, not even, to my eternal shame, myself. Indeed, his absence was only noted when Francis totted up several days worth of takings and realised three hundred dollars were missing from the poke.

It is a cardinal sin to steal from the Kingdom family. The code is quite clear on that point. Opinion quickly hardened against Benji, who was the obvious culprit. Some said he was a bad seed, that he had no place on the show, that he thought he was too good for us. His enraged father fuelled such loose talk, going so far as to suggest that the boy might not be his son. Evalisse remained silent, afraid of her husband.

The Kingdom was in Stawell at the time, near the Grampian ranges, not too far from the South Australian border. It was assumed, because the highway to Melbourne ran through the town, that the thirteen-year-old had jumped on a bus or hitched a lift in that direction. Francis had friends in Melbourne and, after alerting them to keep watch for the runaway, set out in hot pursuit.

My instincts told me he had chosen a different path. I requisitioned some sturdy walking boots and drove to the nearby hamlet of Halls Gap, at the foot of the mountains.

Cathy and I had hiked its trails many years before and I fancied young Benji would be up there somewhere, gazing out over the landscape, seeking perspective. He was not equipped for life in the city, not yet. Terrible to say, I know, but I understood him better than his own father did.

After conducting enquiries at the ranger station, I established that a young fellow matching Benji's description had been seen lurking around the youth hostel in town. When asked, he had claimed to be eighteen, but no one was convinced. The ranger assumed I was his father come to take him home. I almost said that I was. Instead, I claimed to be his uncle and, without going into too many details lest suspicion be aroused, politely asked for the lad's whereabouts.

He had come in that morning for a map and some advice on what trails were open. I was familiar with the one he had chosen and, after reassuring the anxious staff at the information desk that they had done nothing wrong and all would be well, set out to follow in his footsteps.

The ascent was steeper than I remembered, or perhaps it was simply the additional fifteen years of wear and tear on my legs that made a difference. I was not in as good a shape as I once had been, but then what man in his early forties is? It was a weekday, so I had the trail to myself. The sun was warm but not unbearably so, and after the first hour I almost forgot the purpose of my mission, so calm and relaxed had I become.

Benji was at the summit lookout point, a vertiginous platform jutting out from the rock face. He shook his head and laughed when he spotted me, likely relieved to see a friendly face rather than his father's warped countenance. I waved a greeting and clambered up over the final rocks to join him. I was so out of breath I could not say anything for the first few moments. The view was stupendous.

'Do you have any water?' he asked me.

'You didn't set out on this climb without water, did you, Benji?'

'No, I just ran out.'

I disapproved of his lack of preparation more than the fact he had been missing for several days. I handed him a bottle from my pack. He gulped at it eagerly.

'Evidently you were never a boy scout.'

'Evidently.'

We sat together in contented silence. I almost felt like taking a nap. A plume of smoke was rising into the sky some fifty miles distant, a rich amber glow at its base. A bushfire, too far away for us to be concerned about our safety.

'How's Mum?'

'Upset, of course. But it's your father you should be worried about, old chap.'

'Ah, fuck him.' He immediately blushed. 'Sorry, Huw.'

I should say I have never had much tolerance for swearing: not out of prudishness but more the lack of imagination that the use of such blunt words exhibit. In that respect I was a lone voice on the Kingdom, where the vernacular tended towards sentences being lavishly, and I had to admit in some cases quite creatively, peppered with expletives by all and sundry, my own wife included. Demotic, if deficient.

'He assumed you would be in Melbourne by now.'

'But you knew better, eh?'

'I had a notion. You weren't that hard to find.'

'He'll give me a hiding when he gets hold of me.'

'We'll see. Have you spent much of the money?'

'Nah, about a hundred bucks on food and that.'

'It is my solemn duty to remind you of the code...'

'I know, I know. I just had to get away from there, that's all. I'll pay it back.'

'Perhaps you're missing the point.'

'I'm not staying there, you realise. First chance I get, I'm gone.'

'I know that, Benji, much as it saddens me. Where will you go?'

'I was thinking the army.'

'Now why on earth would you do such a foolish thing?'

'Travel overseas. Maybe get a diploma or something. Reckon they're the only ones'll have me. It's not like I'm good for anything else.'

'You underestimate yourself.'

'Nah, you overestimate me, Huw.'

'The Kingdom would find a place for you. There are always new attractions to manage. And I will have to retire one day. Perhaps you could take up my mantle, so the name of Voltan may live on.'

'No offence, but I don't think I'm cut out for what you do.'

'Well, the offer is there, my boy. I would suggest you throw down some ballyhoo for me, but I think it unlikely that Francis would release you from your penury on his stall.'

'Fucken Target Ball. Sorry, but that game's the fucken bane of my life.'

'And yet it is to there that you must return. Will you come back to the Kingdom with me today, Benji?'

'Do I have a choice?'

'Of course. There's always a choice. We could both jump, no?'

We peered over the edge. It was a long way down. Wisely, he chose to accompany me instead. Matters were not that desperate.

The descent through the valleys of granite was cool and pleasant. We talked of many things, mostly of Benji's desire to see the world, to feel like he belonged somewhere. By the time we reached the car, he had me half convinced that his joining the army was a good idea after all. If only I had known then what I do now, I could have gently dissuaded him during the subsequent years, instead of being complicit in his plans. I could have spared him his disfigurement, his fall. Of all feelings, the one I fear most is regret—not for what I did, but for what I may have failed to do.

Upon our return to the Kingdom, Benji's mother scolded him, but not seriously so, for in Francis's absence she sought every opportunity to ingratiate herself with her son. Although there was no great love between them, neither was there animosity. His contemporaries on the show were less forgiving, and he would have faced a tough time of it in the subsequent weeks had it not been for his father's gross overreaction when he got back from Melbourne.

My good friend Boris the strongman alerted me to the fracas. Cathy and I were relaxing in our trailer when he burst through the door.

'Francis is killing Benji,' was all he said, and that was enough. I rushed to the scene. A small number of hands had gathered outside the Target Ball stand, which was locked from the inside. The sounds of a brutal beating emanated from within, punctuated by Francis's vile epithets as he cursed his errant son.

Those present were reluctant to intervene, as this would constitute a breach of the code, but I felt no such compunction. For the first time in years I was overcome by a powerful fury, fuelled by indignation. I had known Francis would clip the boy hard round the ear a few times, but this was going too far. Boris assisted me in breaking down the door, though it was not until I shouted at Francis to desist that he paid us the slightest attention.

'Mind your own fucken business,' he growled, and to my astonishment drove another kick into the curled-up body of his young son. Boris grappled him from behind and within seconds had him locked securely in a full nelson.

I knelt to assess the boy's wounds. He looked up at me, glossy-eyed.

'I told you, Huw.'

Boris held Francis tightly as I towered over him, barely

controlling my rage. To the astonishment of all present, including myself, I threatened to kill him if he ever laid a finger on Benji again, or on his wife for that matter. In for a penny...

Well. That is perhaps an exaggeration—a habit of mine, I admit. What I actually said was that if there were any further incidents of violence towards his family he might one day unwittingly discover the light switch in the Target Ball stand had developed faulty wiring and was live with current. Thirty milliamps is sufficient to stop a man's heart. I am the Master of Electricity, after all.

Francis lost any friends he had that day. Despite Benji's defiance of the carnival code, sympathies on the Kingdom rapidly shifted in his favour. It was his father who was largely shunned by the community. At best, he was treated with suspicion and great caution. He did not seem to care. I felt sorry for Evalisse, trapped in a relationship with such a coward, but there was little that could be done for her. At least he never struck her again, the silver lining to the storm cloud. I have not threatened anyone in such a manner since, nor do I ever wish to again. In any case, I'm not such a terrifying prospect these days.

To his credit, Benji continued to work the Target Ball stand for another few years. He never ran away again and concentrated instead on attaining the basic requirements for entry to the armed forces. I assisted him in this when and however I could. In his spare time he built up his body and by the time he turned eighteen he could almost have taken over from Boris, so fine a physical specimen had he become. He was utterly driven to escape, and he did, eventually, at least for a while.

I missed him, after he was gone. I still do. Benji—the boy who grew up on the carnival, with a cruel bastard for a father and a sword-swallowing erotic dancer for a mother. His path was always destined to be a strange one. He left the Kingdom for good, one fateful autumn day, and he died, that boy, in some foreign desert. I mourn his passing when I think of him. Someone else came back, you see—a man none of us knew, a man utterly changed, a young prince returned from the great war of our time to reclaim his throne. For what, after all, is a Kingdom without a king?

Benji summarily commandeered the Target Ball stand upon his return, forcing Evalisse and Francis into an early retirement, of sorts. They moved into a cottage on the outskirts of Castlemaine, the rent for which was paid for in full by Benji. His mother must have been quietly relieved to be out of the sideshow—as a dancer, she was a shadow of her former self. Through time, her performances had become increasingly lewd and melancholy. Francis protested, but did not press the issue. One look from his son was enough to stifle any complaints. Benji's appearance was positively monstrous. No one pressed him for explanations.

Initially, I was moved by Benji's sudden devotion to his parents' well being. Although he kept his own counsel, I assumed he had returned from his trials an honourable man, wishing to do the right thing.

I soon came to realise this was not the case. His takeover of Target Ball was not done in the spirit of honour or duty. There was an air of spite about his actions, as if he were punishing his parents by snatching away their livelihood, thus rendering them dependent upon him for an income. This Benji had about him the aura of the mercenary.

With Francis and Evalisse out of the picture, Target Ball began to thrive. There was open evidence of a considerable amount of money being generated through the stall. A new element frequented the attraction, and they all walked away with a prize. Giraffes, wombats, kangaroos—all these creatures were eschewed in favour of the blue koala.

I may be an old fool, but I am not stupid. I know that Ben saw an opportunity in Target Ball that his father most likely considered, in his day, but dared not countenance for fear of violating the code and risking expulsion from the Kingdom. The stall had become a mobile base of operations for some shady business venture. Whatever Benjamin had learned in the army, whatever he acquired a taste for in the desert, he now applied to civilian life. His pursuit of this newfound interest was enacted with a ruthlessness that was frightening to witness.

In the past, a council would have investigated any nefarious business affairs that risked bringing the good name of the Kingdom into disrepute, with the perpetrator facing possible censure. No such committee was convened to deal with the situation at Target Ball. Everyone was wary around Benjamin, and chose to remain silent, although fear was also a powerful factor. It is so easy for the blind to see nothing.

More and more, Benji began to resemble his father, although, in many ways, he had become something much worse than Francis. He was a tyrant, resourceful and determined, and his reign over the Kingdom was absolute.

The past may be lost to me, but I no longer harbour any doubts as to what the future holds. Our history is replete with examples of what occurs when an individual becomes obsessed with the acquisition of wealth and power. When he falls, and he surely will, ruination awaits us all, and perhaps we deserve it.

It doesn't really matter, in the end. I won't remember any of it. If I am still alive in twenty years, God help me, and I sit down to look over these words, it will be akin to reading a book of someone else's life. The Kingdom, Voltan, little Benji—I will recall nothing of their exploits. We will be crumbling statues in some antique land, edges worn smooth by the desert winds, forgotten.

MEKONG DELTA

1

Yo, Mekong Delta don't just sit back an' watch
Imma bad motherfucker, leave you holding your
  crotch
You ain't got crabs, girl, that there's the Midas touch
Mekong Delta in da house, just kicked it up a notch.

It be mad boring driving in this country. The radio in Steph's car is cheeks, you can't even get Triple J and it's not like Star FM plays much in the way of Oztang. It's all fucken ads and little-girl pop music and I mean where in the name of fuck'd they get those DJs? Pop a couple of caps in those fake-ass motherfuckers, do the world a favour.

Heads up, here comes the big city of Nowra. Woo, now we're rollin'. Heard there was some dinosaur I oughta speak to, might be able to assist me with my transportation situation. And sho' nuff that must be the place over there with all the broke-ass old cars piled up in stacks and a couple of decent looking rides parked out front. Hard to port, captain, or is it starboard—I never did know the diff. Damn, boy, check out the rims on that Commodore. Oldie but a goodie. Gold paintjob, too. That'll do nicely. Ride be *pimpin'*.

> *Jay-Z may be content to cruise around in his Bentley,*
> *An' that's the kinda dope ride I'll entertain*
> *eventually,*
> *But an Aussie hip-hop artist's gotta remain hardcore,*
> *Hit the blacktop behind the wheel of a fucken*
> *Commodore.*

Stegosaurus comes out wiping his hands on the old oily rag, got a beard on him like Osama bin Laden an' he's wearing a pair of denim dungarees just like the ones I always wanted 'cept you just gots to be rockin' those bad boys barechested. Clocks me eyeballin' the golden chariot an' shakes his head as if to say no way, Keyser Söze, you ain't got the chedda for wheels like that, so throw that shit out yo' head, boy. Changes the fucken record an' flips to the B-side when I flash my roll. Smiles like Christmas come early an' says I can drive her on out of there for three bills straight up. Tell him he's dreamin', dawg. Ride be trill an' all but I mos def gots goods to exchange, you feel me?

Speak fucken Australian.

Damn, what's a gangsta s'posed to do? The revolution hasn't yet penetrated the heart of this country and in the absence of Google Translate I was forced to dumb it down for the ageing motherfucker.

I'll give you the Datsun, plus two grand.

That wasn't even worth a thousand when it was new.

Datsun plus two-five. Come on, you're breaking my heart here. I've had that car since I was a teenager.

Yeah? I've got a violin out the back somewhere.

Fucking hell, it's worth two-fifty at least.

Crazy old coot licks the underside of his moustache with a rank tongue I never want to see again but the deal is done, biatches, an' I rolls on out of there behind the wheel of My First Commodore. Beast. *Got me ninety-nine problems but a Holden ain't one.*

Snoop-a-loop, I can't tell if I'm listing to port or starboard here. I'm all over da joint. It's like the end of *2001* up in my dome. Just what do you think you're doing, Dave? *Daisy, Daisy, give me your answer, do. I'm half crazy, all for the love of you.* Don't get high on your own supply. That's what the man said. Son, you do not want to meet Tony Montana's little friend. That glass highway is one slippery road to perdition an' I be trippin' right the way along that particular stretch of the light fantastic. Alakazam brother, alakazam.

I shouldn't have done it. I shouldn't have done it. I shouldn't have done it. But I done it. Just a little sample of the goods Freddy ever so kindly served up for me. A tiny, teensy-weensy taste, just a wafer-thin mint, monsieur, hardly a trifle. And then bam! The back of a hand across my cheek to rattle the fillings. Bam! But I did floss, I did, just like you told me! Bam! Do you have the faintest fucken idea how expensive Listerine is? That shit's like ten dollars, man. Bam! The dilithium crystals cannae take much more of this, captain, I might have to eject the warp core.

Now you listen to me, mister, and you listen good: you are not ejecting any core of mine and the only tunnel I be going down is track nine to Cooch Central. All aboard, have your tix an' dix in hand, please, gentlemen. Those of you with smaller appendages may assemble in the front carriage. Please be advised there is no dining car so I hope you are prepared to eat out. Holy Jesus fucken Christ our Lord and saviour Allah Buddha Krishna L. Ron Hubbard and Odin as played by Sir Anthony motherfucking Hopkins a little help over here dawg, think I'm drowning I'm waving I'm dying I'm dying and hold your breath and...

Stop.

Exhale.

Open. Your. Eyes.

Rumours of my death have been greatly exaggerated. And I clearly should not do crystal meth when I'm on meds. No. Definitely not. Mos Def. Talib Kweli. Now I know. At least I know. It's not even a question of getting high on my own supply. I just cannot do that shit. Evidently. Indubitably. Holy fuck, that was intense. No wonder the rubes are snatching it up. But it ain't for me, dawg. No sirree, Bob. Or Freddy. Sorry, brother. Freddy. You got a bathroom somewheres

I could use? Oh, and I'll take seven grand's worth. Yup. Seven. Three zeros, homie. Ain't my money. That belongs to Emperor Ming. One and the same. Don't ask, don't tell, don't die foolish. Hey, nice pool!

On top of everything else I gots me a bad case of wit delay. You know, the tendency to think of something abso-fucken-lutely hilarious to say about half an hour after it matters? Yeah, I got that shit like swine flu.

So there's me, hanging in someone's crib at a bangin' party with a bunch of hotties an' maybe we seen each other around but we ain't been properly introduced and every motherfucker with a nut sack is trying to give the impression he's the most suave and sophisticated Homo sapien who ever walked the earth by spouting witticisms at an increasingly frenetic fucken rate. The hilarity level gets raised to giddying heights and then, finally, all eyes fall upon yours motherfucking truly to blow everyone else away with the ultimate, conversation-ending, piss yo' pants gem of pure unbridled flow.

That's when I come undone, that's when the rhymes come up short and I mutter something banal and obvious under my breath and all the beautiful people eyeball each other in sympathy for the sad little goon in the corner who just couldn't raise his game to compete at the highest level of intellectual jocularity an' sink that three-pointer.

Me, I think of that shit thirty minutes later when I's

washing my hands or sitting in the back of a taxi.

Way I heard it, your father is your uncle, yo' rhyme's from the era of Simon and Garfunkel. Which, y'know, when taken out of context makes no fucken sense whatsoever. All I gets for my trouble is a cautious look in the rear-view by the driver, instead of the outpouring of accolades from the crowd, the coy looks from hotties with their skirts hanging so low on their hips you can practically see the crizatch of the snizatch, and the slaps on the back by handsome cavaliers, motherfuckers shaking their heads as they assure everyone that Mikey Dempster is indeed a total fucken crack-up.

It's a debilitating condition. I probs should've had my own stand-up gig or reality show by now. Instead here I is in the back seat of what is admittedly a badass set of wheels, wishing I had a blanket an' hoping no Five-O come moseying along to see what I's doing. Found me a spot off the highway to bunk down for the night but you never know who comes a sniffing. Fucken *Wolf Creek* shit keeping me awake. That an' the meds. I's back on the Risperidone again since 'the incident' at Freddy's place. I don't like taking that shit 'cos it dampens my flow, stops me from coming up with mad rhymes. But the longer I'm clean, the worse it gets up in my dome. Freakaloid detritus strewn all over my brain pan, man. You got your delusions, your psychosis, your disordered thoughts and speech, an' that's just for starters. Word salad, the doc said I had, residual schizophrenia, which ain't as bad as the worse kind but still, monkey be on my back like I'm

Charlton Heston. *Get yo' damn dirty paws off me, simian motherfucker.*

I gots me so much crystal in the trunk that I'm going down for thirty years if the Five-O collars me. Personal use ain't gonna cut this particular brand of mustard. Won't be no tearful scenes in the visitor's room at Barwon for me, neither. I'll end up being the bitch for some big muscly Corporal Wallace motherfucker.

Speaking of which, that cat ain't such a mewling little kitty after all. Bitch got *claws.* Probs not the smartest move buying glass from one of his crew but think I parlayed the deal without raising suspicion. Seven large in cash might be nuff for him to zip it but even so, that solja boy got peeps all over, much more'n I figured. Motherfucker be running half the damn labs on the east coast an' now here's me stuck with a fucken Coles bag full of his product. How'm I supposed to sell this to the rubes and tweakers without him hearing 'bout it? Thinking of driving all the way back to Freo and offloading it there but it be a long, lonely road to the Rinehart, *mein Führer,* and the C-dore ain't exactly easy on the go-go juice.

Go north, young man, go north. That Morgan Freeman in my head always knows what to do. Brisvegas it is, then— the glitz and glamour, the sandflies, the hollow-eyed and desperate. Gots to be the perfect market for a gentleman such as myself looking to offload several kilos of the finest crystal methamphetamine dollars can buy. Wrinkled squinters be lining up to sample my wares, fo' shiz. Camp out in the

Valley and that shit be gone in a week or three, way 'fore the freaks on the Kingdom roll into town.

I be a phantom by then, ghosting back on down to Melbourne high over their heads, leaving on a Jetstar, best seat money can buy, extra legroom an' all that shit. All those motherfuckers will ever hear of me will be my legend.

There's only two places that matter in this world—inside and outside. I'm inside. Everybody else is outside. That's what my moms done told me and damn if she didn't drive that stake right the fuck through the pale, frigid chest of Edward Cullen. You is on your own in this life, dawg. People drift in an' drift out but when you close your eyes at night, it's just you in there. My moms learned that the hard way. She had me real young an' she weren't supposed to have no bambinos at all the doctors said, on account of her being epileptic. That's some scary motherfucking shit right there, homes.

Never forget the first time I seen her fit. Must've only been four or something an' we was having a picnic on the grass near some old stone bridge. Forgot the time an' she didn't have her shades on when the sun was going down. Light come in real low from the horizon and zapped her in the eyes and next thing you know, bam, she hits the dirt like she's been shot by a sniper and goes all stiff, her back archin' and blood coming out her ear 'cos she whacked her head. Lucky my pops knew what to do an' held me back from going to her. You just gotta wait till it passes, ain't nothing

else to do 'cept make sure she's not in danger like if she fell
in the water or the road or somethin'.

Asswipe weren't my pops after all, I just didn't know it
at the time. Weren't till he run out on her that she told me
he was just my stepdad and that she didn't know who my
real daddy was. She had a fit one day coming home from
high school and some rat-fuck piece of shit must've seen his
chance and dragged her in the alley to have his way with her.
When she come out of it one half her uniform was up round
her ears and the other round her ankles. She knew what'd
happened but couldn't remember none of it. A blessing of
sorts, maybes, just like me.

Dude got no idea. Or maybe he does. Probs some boy
from F-Town who knowed her an' just kept his trap shut
when he seen her belly bulging. Always figured that even
though I don't know the prick, he probs knows me. Just ain't
never said shit about it. Fucken coward. He comes forward
some day he better be packing a gat or I'll be chroming that
dome, fo' realz.

Anyways, nuff of that serious shit. Sorry, dawg, this grass
makes me maudlin. Is this a party or what, homes? Pass me
up one of those Bundy an' Cokes an' change the channel.
It's elimination night, yo. Wanna take a bet on the colour
of Matty Preston's cravat? I say purple. If I's wrong, I'll give
you a point, FOC. What? Free of charge, motherfucker.
Shit. An' if I'm right, I get to bust a nut on your clock. Ah,
now chill man, chill, I'm only joshing ya, serious, serious,
I'd never do such a thing, swear on that Gideon Bible in the

drawer there. No, honestly, it was just a joke, sit down will ya, I already paid for the night an' this weed ain't smokin' itself. I just wants some company and you seem like an okay dude. Real purty mouth, too. Nah, nah, hold on, sit the fuck down, will ya, it's only—aha ha, ha ha ha, you should've seen the look on your face, you'd of done it for two points though, right? Aha ha, ha ha ha.

Come on, put on Ten, you'll know it's the right one 'cos of all the flames. Hey, I tell you 'bout the show I'm gonna pitch to these guys? It's like a cross between *Masterchef* and *Survivor*, I call it *Cook for Your Life!* Yeah, now just imagine me up on the screen there instead of Gary, wearing a real dope suit, Armani maybes, an' cue the title music, written by me, natch, an' the camera comes swooping down to a close up of my face just as the beats tail off.

Yo yo Australia, and welcome to *Cook for Your Life!* the show where gourmet cooking really is a matter of life or death! I'm your host, Michael Mekong Delta Dempster, your friendly neighbourhood chart-topping lyricist with a mad flow. For those of you who missed last night's episode, here's the scoop. Our panel of judges decided to really up the stakes for our death-row inmates and challenge them to a taste test of their very own maximum-security-prison beef stroganoff.

Sound easy? Far from it, ladies. With only nine contestants remaining out of the original dozen murderers, paedos and West Coast supporters, the trick is to name all thirty-six of the ingredients in the prison stew. The first person to get one wrong will be eliminated from the competition imme-diately, and eliminated from life itself shortly after.

Yes, that's right, folks—straight from the kitchen to the electric chair! Out of the frying pan and into the fire! Who will guess wrong? Will it be viewer favourite Tricia Q who finally meets the grim reaper? Tricia's notorious of course for going postal at the DFO in Essendon and trying to gun down a dozen of her fellow bargain hunters. Or will it be not-so-gentle giant Bubba Tanning, the cop killer we all love to hate, despite the awesome juniper-crusted beef carpaccio with fig and chilli vinegar that he wowed our judges with last week? All will be revealed on tonight's sizzling episode of *Cook for Your Life!* sponsored by Handee Ultra towels, absorbing even the toughest bloodstains after you've shivved someone in the showers.

Oh, and the last chef standing gets a cookbook deal, a hunnerd large and a pardon from the judge. Dude, the ratings will be *intergalactic*.

2

Gots me the stamina of a dromedary,
Fightin' claws of a crested cassowary,
A vocabulary so extraordinary
They call me the human dictionary.
My flow is so revolutionary
Sometimes I just speak in binary,
One zero one zero one zero one,
That's certainly out of the ordinary.
I'm so hot my nickname is January,
My lap is where bitches seek sanctuary.
My position ain't doggy, it's missionary,
Wanna bust a nut not a capillary.
Won't see me readin' books in no library,
Ain't no fun when you're on your solitary.

This shit is real dawg, it ain't imaginary,
You say literary, I say unsanitary.
Now my secretary say my itinerary be arbitrary,
On the contrary this tour gonna be legendary.
This mercenary attitude of mine be hereditary,
This one's on me, son—don't thank me, it's
   complimentary.

Probs some truth in there at the end. Keep thinking Freddy's gonna grass me up and Corporal Wallace will let his dogs off the leash. Gots to keep off the main roads and away from any kind of town where the motherfucker might have eyes. It's a long way to Brisvegas when you're touring the cockroach byways of New Southey. It's gonna take me fucken forever to get there.

   Least in these small towns there's always a couple of tweakers looking to score or teenagers willing to skim fifty bucks from their mum's purse just so's they can try something new. Don't exactly feel too proud of myself selling them crank but I gots to raise some chedda somehow since I done spent up big on supply. I'm in and out of places so fast I don't even clock their names. Roll up to a milk bar in the C-dore, scope who's lurkin', jaw with them for a while to get the lay of the land, cement some deals an' then bounce. Figure even if one of Ben's crew eyeballs me an' makes the call, I be already gone 'fore I gets braced. Gonna be lookin' over my shoulder everywhere I go for the next month though, paranoid as a fucken andy-roid. Sooner I can cash in and kick back on down to M-Town, the better.

Maybes I shouldn't have left Freo in the first fucken place. Sick of my stepdad, but. Couldn't stand another thirty minutes with the...shit, I almost called him a motherfucker but I can't, I can't be using that particular favourite phrase of mine when I talks about him. It's an accurate fucken description of what he's specifically doing, sexually and otherwise. Asshole be fuckin' her *and* fucking her up. Worst kind of twofer.

Now I gots wheels I'm of a mind to head back over there an' wait for him to come stumbling out the RSL some Friday night, clock the cunt right in the dome with a bat, bundle him into the boot of the C-dore an' head on out to the cliffs at Blackwall Reach. Drunks always be falling or jumping off there so ain't nobody'd bat a fucken eyelid to find his bloated body washed up on the beach a week later, all ate by sharks an' shit. Sure, Mum would cry at his funeral but she'd get over it and ain't nobody who saw the bruises on her face wouldn't be thinking he didn't have it comin'.

Thank fuck he can't get her pregnant. Way I heard it, she got her tubes tied after she had me an' didn't have much choice in the matter. Fucken violation of a woman's rights if you ask me but she had the epilepsy real bad back then and the surgeons, those fucken butchers, advised she be sterilised in case of a repeat incident. When I was old 'nuff to understand, she told me they wanted to flush me right on out of her belly too at the time but she weren't having none of that shit.

Had her hands full anyways with my stepsisters. After

135

my first stepdad run out, she had a couple of boyfriends but nothing serious until Tony come along with his instant fucken family, straight out the packet just add hot water, homes. He seemed all right at first. Had a tragic story and two girls he was strugglin' with, boo friggen hoo. Ended up stopping with us for most of my teenage life. Got me into the Dockers, at least, I'll give the fucker that. Tried out for them himself when he was younger but didn't make the grade.

Was in the army too there for a while, but that didn't last either. Don't know what happened to him, it's not like he got barbecued in Afghanistan like Corporal Wallace or anything. He never even shipped out overseas. Always figured he must've been getting harassed or something and come up short when it was time to kick back. Probs ended up as someone's bitch in the showers. Whatevs. All I knows is he washed out and came on home ready to show us what they'd taught him to do with his fists.

Mum copped it the worst, but I weren't far behind. Tried fighting back but that just made him angrier. Broke couple of my ribs one time an' his precious girls had to step up and put theyselves in harm's way just to make him stop. Please, Daddy, please. They was all right, I s'pose. Didn't have much in common with them since they was a couple years younger than me and into really bad music but least they stuck up for me a few times, though it was probs just so their precious dad didn't wind up in the joint.

Matters got serious once they started growing titties. Tony got real paranoid that I was eyeing them off. Like I'd be remotely interested in diddlin' my own sisters. Fucken maniac. Never knowed the truth of it but I always suspected there was somethin' funny goin' on with him and the girls. They was creepy together and you don't need to be no Dr Freud to work out all those unnecessary warnings he done doled out to me were as much for his own fucken benefit as mine.

Tried convincing Mum to bounce but she was scared, dawg. Scared to leave, scared to speak up. Can't fucken win with assholes like that. Only thing they understands is the way of the gun. One of these days, I swear, I'm gonna go *Halo* on that motherfucker and then that's the one thing he won't never be no more, fo' reals.

Yo yo viewers, this is your host Michael Mekong Delta Dempster broadcasting from a secret location deep within the bowels of the Channel Ten studios. Welcome to tonight's episode of *Cook for Your Life!*—the show where food poisoning just might be a blessing! After last night's shock exit for serial murderer Brian Percy—and believe me, folks, no one was more shocked than Brian himself—we're down to eight remaining contestants on Australia's favourite cookery show. Fair to say Brian was not one of our most loved chefs, having killed his family and two neighbours with an axe and grated their parts into a ratatouille, but he's history now and the relatives of the dead can rest easy in the knowledge he ended up as human toast. Brian was the first contestant to guess incorrectly in last night's sudden-death taste-test elimination when he claimed one of the ingredients he could taste in the stew was 'my wife, Caroline'. Burn!

God, that's hilarious. People would *totally* watch that.

I know, right? 'Cept we don't have the death penalty in Australia, so I'd have to tweak the format a little.

Maybe they could bring it back just for the show?

Maybes, yeah. Hey, you good for a drink? Barkeep, yo, 'sup dawg, can we gets a couple more alcomoholic beverages over here? 'Nother Bundy and Coke for me and a Lemon Stoli for the lady. Nah, no ice, brother, up to my eyeballs in that shit. Anyways, you was sayin' before 'bout leavin' all this behind?

God yeah. Mudgee's a sweet little town and everything but it's so boring. There's, like, nothing to do here unless you're into playing pool while morons like Jackie Dawson pretend to do you from behind with his cue. He's so immature. Typical country boy.

Romance is dead. Dudes like that, man, all they want is a root in their ute.

Eww.

I feel you. So where you headed? Sin City?

I was thinking maybe Newcastle. What about you?

Brisvegas. Gots me some merchandise I needs to offload. After that I'll be sweet for cashola for, like, two years.

Wow. Maybe you can pitch the idea for your cooking show to the TV people then. You know, I've got a couple of ideas myself, not for shows though, just stuff that doesn't exist yet.

Yeah? Pitch 'em to me, sugarish.

No way. I don't want you stealing them.

I just told you 'bout my show, right? And how 'bout this—for every idea you tell me, I'll run another one of mine by you. And we drink to celebrate what fucken geniuses we are.

Ha ha—okay, well, don't laugh but how come we don't have fluoro black yet?

How's that work?

It's like a material you make clothes from. It's black but when someone shines a light on it, it goes fluoro.

That would look dope in a club.

Yeah, I guess. I was thinking more so that cars could see you walking home at night.

Oh yeah, safety, safety, that's trill. How come we don't got that? One of those Jean Paul Gaultier motherfuckers oughta bring that out. Yo, listen up, I gots another one. Picture this—a brand-new sport called SK8Ball. Capital S, capital K, number eight, then 'ball' with a capital B. It combines two of the most popular street sports of the last hunnerd years: basketball and skateboarding.

How's it played?

On a court the size of a footy field that looks like a massive skate park. You got a black volleyball-sized ball with the number eight on it, that's the eight ball like in pool, and you gotta ride your deck over the terrain and pass the ball around in your team, then try to sink baskets that are placed in fiendish spots to reach. I figure the easiest basket is worth three points, let's call it a 'trip', then the next hardest is worth five points, we call that one a 'cinch' and the hardest one to sink is worth ten, that's a 'dixie'. Or maybe a 'doozy', I ain't decided yet. You gots to be a Tony Hawk-style motherfucker to score a doozy, though.

That's so cool. It sounds really dangerous.

Shit yeah, but can you imagine the combos? Guys doing verts while some other motherfucker tries to knock them off and steal the ball? Fucken awesome.

Aww, yours are way better than mine. The only other thing I can think of is a Meminto, and there's no way that can even exist.

A Meminto? Pray tell, m'lady.

It's like Mentos, except when you suck it you get information that goes into your brain, just simple stuff like someone's phone number.

Whoah. Full on! So like you's out on a date with someone and you kinda like them and stuff so you give 'em a breath mint at the end of the night and your phone number gets zapped into their brain somehow?

Exactly! Plus, if you want to pash them, you know they've got minty fresh breath.

Fuuuck. I'll raise a glass to that. I thought I was mental but that is straight up off-the-hook *beast*. Nice work. Get on to Apple about that shit.

Oh wait, I just remembered another one.

Hold up, girl, it be my turn now.

This is fun.

A'ight, a'ight, so this one's for the man who travels a lot, like your salesmen and backpackers and shit. I call it the Razorbrush. It's a disposable razor with a toothbrush at the other end of the handle. Bam!

Wait, doesn't that exist already?

Never seen one. Don't think so.

Huh. You'd think it would though, right? Seems obvious.

S'what I'm sayin'.

You could have one for women too. Keep the teeth clean and the legs smooth.

Not just the legs.

Hmm. No comment.

What's your other idea?

Oh yeah. I was thinking how good would it be if there was some sort of bead necklace you could wear that would prevent you from drowning. Like if you got tired in the ocean, or caught in a rip, or bumped your head on your surfboard, or just couldn't swim?

What's it made from?

I don't know. Something that hasn't been invented yet. Something super buoyant so your head just can't physically go under the water.

You mean like a lifejacket?

Yeah but no, just a tiny necklace so you don't have to wear a lifejacket all the time. It's pretty lame, but the only thing I could think of calling it was the Float-a-Neck.

Ha ha, yeah, that needs some work. What about Drown-away?

God, that's even worse.

Safety Beads?

Maybe. Hey, if you help me come up with a good name for it, I could cut you in on the profits.

Oh, so we's going into bidness together now, issat right?

Well, you seem like a man who's going places. Rolling into Mudgee in that fancy car of yours, paying for all my drinks, making me laugh, telling me all about your album.

Caused a stir, have I?

More of a stirring, let's say.

I see. On that note, I think it's high time we moved this business discussion to a more amenable location. You know a joint round here we could hang an' not be disturbed?

I know just the place.

Sweet as. Let's bounce, baby.

Breathe it in, that's right, now hold it, hold it…and exhale. You feel it? It's tha bomb, right? You wanna get out of Mudgee, this here's one way, girl, ain't no big city gonna match the hit you get from crystal. But you know, I ain't tryin' to quash your dreams or nothin', just sayin' you gots to be realistic an' also open your horizons so you is ready for life in the land beyond.

You feelin' relaxed now? That's the way, just kick back and take in those stars. Yo, this is good glass, though you gots to be careful you don't get hooked or nothin'. Moderation is the key, girl, the key to everything in the world. Can't be drinkin' too much, can't smoke too much, can't be scarfin' too much red meat—shit, likely only a matter of time 'fore they tells us sex be bad for us too.

It is. You can catch diseases. Are the stars meant to be moving like that?

Ain't no flies on me, girl. Gots me a clean bill of health in that department. Been livin' the life of a monk over here, to tell you the truth.

Sex on ice must be amazing.

Wet and slippery, I hear.

Sounds good. Wait, what do you mean, 'you hear'? You've never done it after smoking?

Me, I gots to be careful with that shit. Though…I'm off meds this week, so fuck it, pass me that pipe, girl…Oh man, that goes straight to the brain stem, don't it though? See what you mean 'bout them stars, maybes we done switched hemispheres an' didn't notice. Hey, you serious 'bout doin' it?

Sure. Why not? Nobody ever comes down to this old dam, the water level's too low for swimming.

Ain't got no flunkies, though.

Don't worry about it. I've got one of those implant thingos.

The pizatch for the snizatch? Music to my ears, girl. In that case, I gots me a recipe for your cookbook right here.

You talk funny. Take my skirt off—I can't seem to move.

Panties too?

Yes, but don't call them that. No woman likes that word.

Fo' reals? But that's what they always say in the movies an' shit.

I know. Nah. Horrible word.

What you prefer, then?

Undies. Knickers, maybe.

Knickers, yeah, I like that. Duly noted. Oh wow, that's, uh, that's fucken awesome actually.

Is it? I never really know if it's pretty or ugly. I can't see it from that angle.

Take it from me, girl, you look *fine*. That's the sort of cooch should be put up on a pedestal an' worshipped by the masses.

Really? Well then, in that case bow down, my subject.

Oh no, oh no, no no no, this ain't happenin', this can't be happening. Wake up, Debs—wake up, girl. Hold on, Imma pinch your thigh real hard now—shit, watch where you goin', dawg, keep your peepers on the road. Ain't gonna do neither of us no good if you wraps the C-dore round a tree. Holy fuck, look at the size of that welt on her skin an' it didn't even stir her none. This is bad, so fucken bad. What am I gonna do? Can't take her to no hospital, an' even if I could where the fuck's the nearest one round here? We're in the middle of fucken nowhere, needs me a helicopter to get her out of here 'fore she ups and dies on me. Fuck fuck fuuuck, what was you thinkin', Mikey? Letting some small-town girl you just met smoke up a crystal storm. She must've had a reaction or something.

A'ight, a'ight calm down, homes, calm the fuck down, panicking ain't gonna solve this—just get your head straight and think, man, think. Least she ain't dead, her eyelids is still flickerin' an' she be makin' weird noises. Think maybes she pissed herself a little but that's gotta be a good sign, right? So all I gots to do is drop her off somewheres they'll take care of her. Outside someone's house or somethin', ring the bell and drive off 'fore they sees me. Ain't pretty, but that'll have to do it. Can't very well take her to the cop shop, not with all this fucken glass in the back.

Shit, here comes Mudgee now, slow down, slow down, Mikey, can't get pulled over now or attract attention. Keep to the speed limit and look for a place with the lights still on, far side of town next to the road. They's good people in these small towns, someone'll do the right thing. Oh Christ, I'm sorry, Deb, I really am, me and my big mouth and all this talk, always talking I am and it's shit, it's all shit, why'd you have to listen to me? Look at you, girl, look at you there with your head lollin' all over the seat like you is tryin' to find your way back to your body, please don't die, please don't die. I'm sorry to have to leave you like this, no skirt, no panties, I mean knickers, no knickers, everyone'll think you got raped—oh man, can this night get any worse? What a fuck-up, what a total fucken fuck-up, but don't worry they'll take care of you, someone will take care of you and I'm sorry it can't be me—just hold on baby, hold on. Look, here's a place, nice-looking house, garden and everything, lights burning in the lounge, watching *CSI Miami* or somethin', shit's 'bout to get real for them.

A'ight, just pull over real easy there, Mikey, throw 'er in neutral and keep the engine running, that's it, no dramas. Crack the passenger door and sneak on round there, nobody's looking, oh man, this is fucken horrible—what I'm doing— maybes I should just hand myself in but no, no, I can't, I can't do ten or twenty years for this, just for having some fun, it ain't my fault what's happened to you, not really, it's your brain, your brain can't handle the crystal.

I wish I'd not left your skirt behind—makes this look so much worse than it is. But I can't think about that now, I've gotta go, Deb, gotta bounce. An' I promise I won't steal your inventions an' I'll stand on the horn when I leave so's they'll come out an' find you. I hope you don't hate me. I'm sorry, I'm sorry and that's it, baby, I'm in the wind.

3

Hand me one of those controllers, move the fuck over bitches and prepare to have your asses whupped. Playa, playa, multi-playa. Mekong Delta is in da house. Lemme just select my character here. What do I needs to know, control wise? Word me up, dawg. Anything weird?

You played *Call of Duty*?

Fo' shiz. I clocked that shit in a weekend, bra.

This is the latest in the series. *Black Ops*. Same thing, only we're in Vietnam and Cuba.

Beast. Mekong Delta be right at home. Be warned, though, I's gonna wreck you guys instead of the locals. Them's my people, dawg.

You got fucken slope blood in ya, mate?

Lock that racist shit down, motherfucker, 'fore I snatch you out that chair. Ain't no need for that kinda talk. Didn't nobody tell you more Australians got Asian heritage now than European?

Bullshit.

Nuh-uh—look it up, homes, that be the triple truth. This an Asian country you living in now, so suck it up, brother. White folks is a dyin' breed, and good riddance too, I says. Motherfuckers is holding this country back.

You fucken little arsehole.

So you playing or talking, Eminem?

Chillax, dawg, I's just familiarising myself with the controls here an' having a discussion about multiculturalism with your racist-arse friend.

Calling me racist in my own fucken country? Un-fucken-believable. My granddad fought for this country and now it's overrun with fucken Lebbos and wogs and slopes. I'm not racist, mate, no fucken way, but all these people don't belong in Australia.

Yeah? Identify as Indigenous, do you bra?

What? Course I fucken don't.

So do I gots to spell it out for you?

Eh? What's this little prick talking about, Tommo? He doesn't even speak plain fucken English.

Fuck sake, Lachy, stop shouting, we're trying to play here. Your family's Scottish and Dutch, right?

Yeah? So?

Well, then, you came to Australia on a fucken boat just

like every other cunt—that's what he's saying.

Youse two are the cunts. That's a very offensive accusation.

Fuck off outside and cry then, and while you're at it text Matt and see if he's on his way. I want to get this deal done before our guest here takes his business elsewhere because of your fucken prejudices.

All right, I know when I'm not wanted. Pricks.

Sorry about that, mate, he's really into all that stop-the-boats shit. Fucken ice blackened his brain as well as his teeth.

It's a'ight, dawg, they's all the same in these piss-ant towns. Present company excepted, course.

Funny thing is, every time he sees a hot Asian chick he practically jizzes his boardies.

I hear that. Who doesn't, am I right? So you think Matt's gonna give me a good price? I gots some mad merch to offload on you guys.

Totally. Lucky you turned up, actually. There's a serious drought round here at the moment. Matt's cook got sick so he hasn't been able to produce much lately. Good job you came to us first too, instead of trying to sell it directly to the tweakers yourself. Matt's got a bit of a temper on him and this is sort of his patch, you know?

You gots to respect a playa's territory. Me, I'm just looking to cash out of this game. I seen too much already. This life ain't for me, homes, you feel me?

Totally, totally. Hey, you're pretty good at this. Pick up the crossbow, pick up the crossbow!

*

You didn't tell me this cunt was a Dockers fan.

Hold up, you don't barrack for West Coast, do you? Don't know if I could do bidness with no Eagle.

Nah, mate, fuck those wooden spooners, I'm Freo all the way.

Fo' reals? A'ight, that's fucken great news! How d'ya think we'll do this year? Woulda had us a grand final if it weren't for those bitches from St Kilda.

Yeah, least they got done on the big day.

Did you watch the derby?

Did I? Wouldn't fucken miss it, mate. What a day, that's the most we ever beat those Eagle cunts by. I reckon we'll be right this year, maybe take it a step further, eh?

Kick it up a notch, Dockers! *Give 'em the old heave ho!*

Ha ha, you're all right, mate, don't hear many singing that round here.

Man, this is awesome. Make me a good offer and the glass is yours, my friend. I'd be stoked to have a Dockers fan take it off my hands.

Oh, I'll take it, no worries there, mate. How much you got exactly? The boys here told me you reckon you've got quite the stash.

Shit yeah, homes. I got, let's see, 'bout six grand's worth left, that's wholesale price, of course, being as that's what I paid. But I ain't greedy, you know? I'll take ten for it. I mean, I could sell that shit for fifty a point and make myself thirty large but I's kinda in a rush and besides, I wouldn't wanna be sellin' on your corners, right?

That's good business, showing respect like that.

S'what I'm all about, brother. You take care of me and I'll drop thirty gees of fucken awesome glass in yo' lap. Sweet as a honey-roasted nut.

I'll most definitely take care of you, don't you worry about that. Come on then, show us the gear. You got it hid somewhere?

Nah, it's in that Coles bag if you want to check it. It's good product, plenty of satisfied customers.

You brought it in here with you? In that bag?

Fo' sho. We's all good here.

What the fuck makes you think that?

Well, I...wait, what you mean? I haveta bring the product in with me to show you so's you know what you's buying.

Buying? Who said anything about buying? Tommo, quit playing games for a fucken minute and grab a hold of that bag, will ya?

Yo, hold up, motherfuckers, that shit be mine, mine.

You think? Lachy, step in here a minute, mate.

My fucken pleasure, boss. Call me a racist, will ya, ya fucken slope-lovin' little cunt.

Here, show me that bag, Tommo. Ho ho ho, fucken jackpot! Hoy, watch what you're doing there, Lachy. He's bleeding all over the fucken rug. Don't fucken beat him to death neither—I need a new cook and I want him to be able to walk out of here tonight.

Hold on, just one more. Righto, that'll do it. And fucken think twice in future before you call someone a racist, you little prick.

Is that his Commodore outside? Tommo, get the keys out of his pocket and it's yours, mate. Nice work tonight, we've scored big time here.

How come Tommo gets the car? What do I get?

Fuck sake, Lachy, you're such a whinger. Here, take a couple of points of this and smoke it up tonight. Let me know if it's any good. But before you do, drag this piece of shit out to my car. I don't want to get blood on me. Oh and Tommy, I meant to tell you, I got a new game but I forgot to bring it. It's the latest *Assassin's Creed*. Graphics on it are fucken sick, mate.

What do I know about cooking meth? Sweet fuck all but I ain't about to tell this guy that. Gots to play along with what's happening, act like I'm done, I'm beat, then flit on out of this fucken town first chance I gets. Can't believe they took the keys to the C-dore. That ain't right. The glass, a'ight, I sees now I should've been more careful, I don't know what I was thinking rockin' up there and presentin' them with a golden fucken Willy Wonka ticket. I weren't thinking, that was the problem. Too fucked up by what happened to that girl Deb to see straight. Too eager to ditch the glass and get paid. Shoulda drove straight on through to Brisbane and sold it to someone who wouldn't rip me off, someone who knew how to conduct business. But no, you couldn't wait, could you, Mikey? Had to get it sorted now, right fucken now. Shoulda waited, dawg. Shoulda thought things through.

Now this snake-eyed motherfucker got my glass and my ride, and me. My nose is fucken bleeding too where that motherfucker kicked me in the face. Asshole gonna pay for that, fo' reals. Maybes I can turn this situation to my advantage. They's just small-time tweaker scumbags, it ain't like at Freddy's joint with a couple of bikies locking the place down with pitbulls and shotguns. First time they's all out their heads I'll walk on out of there with my glass, my car keys and all their fucken money, maybe throw a match into their lab and do the world a favour at the same time. Can't do this shit on your own, homes. Needs me a gat or a fucken mate or something so's I got some back-up. No honour in this world no more. What's it come to when you can't even conduct a simple business transaction without gettin' boned?

Listen to him lording it over me there like he be some kinda meth king. Doin' me a favour, he says, 'cos we both barrack for Freo. Coulda had me disappeared, he says— but no, he thinks I got potential and that I just needs some schoolin' in the game. Start at the bottom, 'stead of tryin' to be a gangsta straight out the gate. Shit, I gots to get away from these small towns, they is a major irritation to my dome. Everyone think they know where it's at but they don't know jack shit. Plus they all talk like they's Aussie crims from the friggen seventies. Watched too much *Underbelly*. They be all ya farken cunt this, ya farken cunt that, farken wogs and

153

Lebbos—I mean, seriously, dawg? Who talks like that in the second motherfucking decade of the twenty-first century? Ain't you watched a movie or turned on the box in the last thirty years? An' what, you got a thing against the Lebanese? What the fuck is that all about? Gots to be less than a hunnerd thousand of the motherfuckers in the whole damn country an' like, so what? Probs more Germans in Australia than there is Lebanese an' you don't hear nobody bitchin' about them, do ya? Ain't no white folk whining about how the Huns should go back to their own country an' shit.

Course I'm the bad guy for pointing this out. I'm real sick of this shit, man. Sick of gettin' my ass handed to me by low-lifes still livin' in the past, an' not the good past neither, like the one with free love and jazz clubs and steam trains an' shit. What about the future, dawg? Why can't we be lookin' to the motherfucking future? Born in the wrong fucken time, I was.

Damn, can't stop this bleeding. Think maybe that bitch done broke my nose or somethin'. Just keep nodding at whatever this motherfucker be sayin'. Yessir, right sir, absolutely, I agree with you, thanks for the opportunity an' all—I really appreciate it, you thievin' crankhead piece of shit. Oh man, would you just look at this town—they really got it going on here don't they, the joint is jumpin', 'spose the Friday night bingo game is going off right about now. Shit, even if I can't get my hands on my property maybes I'll just leap on the next bus north anyhow and leave this whole sorry situation behind. Fucked if I's stayin' here to cook up meth for this punk-ass motherfucker. Plenty of other things I can do to make some paper. I got mad skills, dawg, don't know why I be wastin' them slummin' it with all these two-bit wannabe gangsters and tweakers eking out a livin' at the bottom of society's barrel. No more foolin' around with crank or any other dirty fucken substance that fucks people up just to increase the size of your roll. I mean, just listen to this asshole layin' down the rules for me like I be his slave now or somethin'. Yessum, massa, tote that barge, lift that bale, you want I should cook you up some grits with that batch of meth, suh? Ow ow ow fuuuck, my face hurts and my back hurts and my nut sack hurts where that ferret-faced fuck sunk the boot in, though thank almighty fuck he weren't wearin' no actual boots, they was just a dirty old pair of Asics runners. Dumb fuck ain't even got no style. Surprised he didn't strip the Nikes off my feet when he was takin' everythin' else I owned.

Yeah, yeah, blah blah blah motherfucker, look at you all pleased with yourself 'cos you got one over on a homeboy. Damn, you got swag now an' is lovin' every minute you gets to put me in my place. Well, enjoy your moment of glory, Matthew, thinkin' you is the end-of-level guardian. Soon as your stinky ass is turned I be ghostin' right on out of Gilgandra or whatever the fuck you calls this sinkhole, an' maybes slippin' somethin' sharp 'tween your ribs just so's you bleed out on the floor of your dirty fucking hovel—see how your rug looks then, motherfucker.

This your street? Fo' reals? Shit, what a streak of misery.

An' don't be sayin' home sweet home to me, motherfucker. Ain't gonna be my home for long an' that's the triple truth, you can be sure of that. Uh-huh, I am *done*. Checked out. Finished. Gonna steal your money just like I done with that damn fool solja boy an' start me a new life in the colonies, 'cept this time I won't make the same mistake by thinking I can use the chedda to ante up to the big time. Nuh-uh, this time I be takin' a right turn off the glass highway.

Don't look back, don't look back, maybe I can make those trees 'fore he sees me, maybe I can find somewhere to hide, cover myself in leaves or something. Just keep going, Mikey, keep those legs pumping and don't think about him, don't think about what he'll do if he catches you. Oh fuck, he's going to catch me, isn't he, he's going to catch me and he's going to fuck me up so bad. Watch where you're going, watch…ah, fucking hell, I can't see for shit out here. Get up, get up and keep going. Maybe there's a road out past those trees, maybe I can flag someone down before he finds me. Gots to get some distance between us.

Fuuuck, he had a gun, an honest-to-God nine milli-metre and he was waiting for us, just sitting there in the dark waiting for us. How did he know I'd be there? He didn't know, he couldn't know, there was no way for him to know. The look on his face, though—oh Jesus, the look on his face when he saw me. Whatever business he had with Matt went straight out the window when he clocked my sorry ass. The solja boy, return of the solja boy.

What the fuck was he doing there? Matt didn't work for him, obviously, not the way he reacted when that lamp came on like in some fucken cheesy thriller where the bad guy's in your house, he's in the fucken house, how did he get in the fucken house and why, why?

Shit, it don't matter why, and it don't matter how. He was there. The big bad wolf, the fucken east-coast meth lord with the map of scars on his face and he couldn't hardly believe what he was seeing, he couldn't believe his own luck. I fell right in his lap and all Matt had to do was keep his head and hand me over, probs would have got a fucken reward but no, that dumb fucken crankhead wannabe-gangsta flipped out when he saw Corporal Wallace sitting there in his lounge room, cool as you fucken like.

As you would, I guess, as you would. Started rantin' and ravin', shoutin' who the fuck are you an' what the fuck you doing in my crib, don't you know who I am, you've no fucken idea who you're dealing with, ya cunt. 'Tween that and Ben not believin' his eyes at me stood there holding my bleeding nose I knowed I had about two seconds to bolt 'fore it all went pear-shaped.

Took to my heels out the front door and all I saw was Ben jumping up so fast his gat slid off his knee. Matt took his shot and lunged at him while he fumbled to pick it up. Didn't seem like an even tussle but Matt had smoked a point 'fore we left the other place an' thought he was fucken invincible. Can't say what happened after that and don't really give a fuck—all I know is whatever's going on back there is keeping Ben occupied, maybes Matt is giving him a run for his money after all. Buying me time, that's all I care about. Maybe I can make it. Shit, I think I'm going to make it.

Stop. Wait. Stop. Was that a…there it is again. That's two. Two shots. Someone got their paws on that nine and loosed off a couple of rounds. Oh man, that ain't good. I got a bad feeling that was Matt going down. If it'd been him picked up the nine he'd of emptied the clip for sure. But it was just two shots. Two shots. One to put Matt down, maybe another to the dome. Kill shot. Double tap. Had to be the solja boy.

The light at the door. The silhouette. The head turning, lookin' my way. Here he comes. Oh Jesus suffering fuck, here he comes. Move, Mikey, move, just run.

The trees the branches the darkness the moon. My legs, oh my legs. I can't breathe, I can't get a breath. Can't stop. Can't stop. He's big. He's so big and fast and fit and strong and he's coming, he's coming, he's in the trees, he's coming. How can he be in the trees already? Which way, which way do I go? Don't shoot me, man, I hope he doesn't shoot me—not in the back, not in the legs, please not in the legs.

I want to see, I want to see it coming if it has to be that way. The one in front of the gun lives forever. It's dark in there, dawg, so dark in that nine-millimetre hole. I don't want that to be the last thing I see. I want to see the sun again, the beach, the cookie jar of a beautiful woman. I got so many recipes I still wanna try, and ideas, I got ideas to give to the world. That all gonna be lost and no one will ever know who I might've been. Forgotten, I'll just be forgotten and that can't be, that's not how it's supposed to be.

Yes, yes, I hear you, I'm stopping, I can't go on anyway. Ben, I give up, I give up. You got me, dawg, and hey look, brother, I'm sorry, I'm so, so sorry. I don't know what I was thinkin', takin' your roll like that. It was a mistake, a terrible mistake. I know that now. I know who you are and please don't shoot me, don't. I'll do anything you want, anything to make it up to you. I'll work Target Ball and hand out those blue koalas to all your customers and more, I'll make more for you, I'll make you all the money just please don't, don't. Oh. Oh, no.

4

A'ight, so things could be worse. I could be six feet under
the gun right now, worms crawling through the eight-ball
haemorrhage in my dome, wombats snuffling my mortal
remains, maybes tryin' on my Nikes for size. Or I could be
staked out in the desert somewheres like I heard the Taliban
done with prisoners, the skin of my belly peeled back. Not
enuff to kill ya, but so you gets to see your guts eaten by
flies and ants and roaches and whatever other dirty fucken
bugs they got over there.

Nah, under the circumstances, think I made out like a
bandit. Well, maybes not that great but it definitely could
be worse, you feel me? I mean, I didn't get shot, not yet
at least, and sure I copped another beating but honestly I

been clocked by so many dudes this past year I done lost count. Whatever happened to usin' your words, boys? A bit of banter, insults traded back and forth, like yo' momma so big her first name be Notorious. Yo' momma so big McDonald's done introduced Yo' Momma Size. Yo' momma so big her map of Tasmania *is* Tasmania.

But naw, motherfuckers don't got no game when it comes to wordplay. 'Stead they be all like, Imma knock your teeth out, cunt. Or, Imma break your fingers, ya little prick. Or, Imma kick you so hard you ain't gonna shit properly for a month. Actually, that last one ain't bad.

Hold up, hold up, I should be payin' attention here. Corporal Wallace is tryin' to impress upon me the reality of my situation. Man, it is so weird being back in the Target Ball stand. It's like I was just here yesterday, 'stead of however many weeks it's been. Course it ain't open for bidness or nothin', not yet anyways. Best the chumps don't see this particular show. Ol' Ben might as well have sold tickets. Bit of a carny crowd gathered and they weren't exactly linin' up to slap me on the back. Caught a couple of hits on the way through 'fore Ben warned the freaks off. Never had me no friends on the Kingdom anyways an' I gots even less now. Get the feelin' this one's gonna be tricky to extricate myself from, fo' reals.

When he tied me to this chair I thought fo' sho' I was gettin' waterboarded or some crazy CIA anti-terrorist shit. At the very least I figured on sayin' a fond farewell to a couple of my toenails. Goodbye, little pinkie! But naw, no torture, no Abu Ghraib shit, not even a knuckle sandwich to chew

on. He ain't touched me, which is kind of a worry. Maybes
he figures I had enough of a beating before. Or maybes the
pliers is comin' out any second, I'm in the dark over here an'
ready for anything. What happened to Matt and his loser
crew anyways? Best not to ask, I guess.

Brung me back here in Steph's old Datsun. Could be how
they tracked me down. Old coot in Nowra musta blabbed.
Don't matter now. I's back on the Kingdom and whatever
Ben says goes. Speaking of which, he be talking numbers.
Better listen up.

Since I recovered most of the glass you bought from that
dickhead Freddy, and he's already refunded the money you
stole, technically you don't owe me anything.

Great news, bra! So if you just wanna loosen these here
bonds, I'll be on my way an' won't trouble you no further,
no sir.

Yeah, I don't think so.

A'ight. So what's the dally-o? You gonna keep me locked
up in here like Fritzl's daughter? Slip my meals under the
door? Come tuck me in at nights?

Pretty much, actually. You're lucky that you're of more
use to me alive than dead. From now on, you'll work Target
Ball and sell product. If you behave, then after a while I
might let you roam the alley, but no further.

So that's it? I's a prisoner on the Kingdom now?

Part of the family.

For how long?

Until I say otherwise. A year, maybe. See how you go.

'Spose I don't need to ask what happens if I goes walk-about?

I advise against it. Put it this way—you're not my first employee.

Last guy got promoted, did he? S'okay, don't answer that, I get it. This here's my crib now, s'all good, yo. I be down with that. You won't get no more shenanigans from me, Ben. After what I been through these past weeks, the quiet life suits me just fine, dawg. Mouth shut, ears open, eyes wide, sales patter ready to roll. Now about these ropes, bra, they's kinda chafin' my wrists.

I'll be back in the morning. You'll start work then.

What, you's leaving me tied up like this all night? Wait, how'm I supposed to perform my, uh, ablutions, y'know?

If you gotta go, you gotta go. Goodnight, Mikey.

Oh, just like that, huh? You ain't gonna give me a bucket or nothin'? A'ight, a'ight, I'll just have to hold it in but I warn you, this could be messy in the morning an'...ah, fuck it, he's gone. Mother*fucker*.

Back to bidness as usual, 'cept I got promoted, kinda. Super-sized. My piece increased. Back in the saddle an' ridin' till dawn. 'Cept this time there be rules a-fucken-go-go.

Fifty a point, huh? An' what if the cracker comes up short? I got any leeway?

Nah. Don't do half points, no matter how much they beg you.

You ain't worried 'bout losing custom?

This isn't Bunnings, Mikey. It's not good customer service and low, low prices that brings them back. Everyone knows it's fifty a point. If they only have forty, they're taking the piss out of you. You have my permission to respond accordingly.

Sweet. So basically I can badmouth these a-holes all I like.

Knock yourself out.

An' I take it we don't do trade.

Such as?

Y'know, hummers and handjobs.

You ever seen inside the mouth of a meth head? I don't think you want to be putting your dick anywhere near that. Besides, you're not here to enjoy yourself.

A'ight, a'ight, I know, it's all about makin' paper.

Treat them like shit. Don't let them get friendly with you. And those fucken rap songs of yours? Keep 'em to yourself. Don't think because you're selling them meth, they're obliged to listen to your fucken lunatic ravings.

That's cold, homes. But a'ight, I'll just follow the advice Bolton gave to Hasselhoff.

You're going to tell me even though I don't want to hear it.

Stick to the ballads, dawg.

No fucken singing at all, Mikey. You're not auditioning for *Australia's Got Talent*. You're selling crystal meth for me, and I will bury you in a fucken shallow grave if you step out of line one more time. You do understand that, right?

In tha dome like a metronome, boss. An ever-present refrain. Ballyhoo the chumps, bitch slap the tweakers, umpire the blue koala zone, eighty-six the bottom feeders and increase the roll. You can rely on me. I ain't going nowhere and ain't doin' nothin' 'cept working this here stall, an' that's the triple truth, Ruth.

Don't fuck it up.

Scout's honour.

And no dipping the product.

Can't do it anyways. Don't mix too well with my meds.

Yeah, those I do want you to take. Only thing seems to calm you fucken down. Steph'll get your prescription filled.

I mights be needin' a little somethin' for my restless leg syndrome too, boss. I gets agimitated if I don't get my drank on once in a while and, well, how do I put this delicately, the occasional flash of cooch sure works wonders for gettin' a man through those long, lonely nights, you feel me?

Fuck sake, I'm not running a strip bar here. Use your imagination—it's vivid enough. And you better not get restless fucken legs.

A'ight, don't get your pantyhose all in a twist. I's just askin'.

Be better off in the joint. Leastways there you gets Foxtel, three squares an' regular blowjobs, though I'd probs have to open wide and stick out the old tongue myself. Not exactly how I dreamed of spending my summer but I'd do it if I had to. It's just jizz after all, ain't hydrochloric acid or nothin'. 'Stead here I be cooped up in this trailer 'bout the size of a hotdog van, nothin' but cuddly toys, tweakers and my own right hand for company, livin' off a steady diet of potato cakes and dimmies from Shark Bites.

What's worse is I have to pretend to like it. Have to keep my lips zipped, take my medication, Nurse Ratched, and watch the sights and sounds and lights and colour and all the fun of the fair flowin' right on by my window. This be it for me, dawg. This be my very own crystal kingdom, and it ain't no fairytale with Goofy on ice skates, fo' reals.

Roll up, roll up, all y'all high rollers! Don't be shy, come on in an' test your mettle on Target Ball, quite likely the easiest game in sideshow alley! We gots prizes galore an' all of them fluffy. Perfect for the kiddlywinks, laydeez, an' gentlemen of a more artistic inclination. Yes, it is as obvious as it sounds, sir, if you've got the balls then I'll give you five more an' all you gots to do is land 'em in the rings to win big, big prizes! Just look at the size of those targets! How can you miss? It's nigh on impossible.

I should point out for legal reasons that the game is in no way related to the chain of popular department stores but don't let that stop you from steppin' up and showin' off your throwin' skills. How 'bout you, sir? You seem like the type of capable gentleman who could clean me out tonight. No? You're sure? Well, that is surprising—I could've sworn you were a master ball manipulator but perhaps you is more used to havin' them in your mouth than twixt yo' fingers—

yeah, that's right, just keep on walking, you didn't even hear what I just said then, did you…what a bunch of chumps and oh, lookee here, what a cute family if you consider extraordinarily prominent foreheads to be attractive, are you two cousins or what, how the fuck'd you wind up with kids that look like they been stitched together from dead bodies, that cannot be natural, homie.

Here we go, finally a clem willing to take the bull by the horns, except oh I see, you a player or a *playa*, dawg? Don't answer that, I can tell from that sticky-looking scrunched up fitty-dollar bill in your paw that you falls into the latter category. Homeboy, I don't even wanna be touchin' that, ain't you got soap in your crib? Never mind, give it here, lucky I gots me a damp rag and a bucket of suds for just this precise reason. Hygiene is paramount, dawg, didn't yo' momma tell you that?

Damn, you gotta admire the Australian mint, makin' their notes waterproof. You know I accidentally washed about five hunnerd dollars one time? Was in the pocket of my work jeans and I done forgot all about it, just came home to my mom's place an' stripped right there in the laundry. Put the whole shebang through the wash cycle and didn't even 'member 'bout the cashola till I opened the lid an' saw all them pineapples plastered round the drum. Damn near soiled my shorts at first, till I realised they wasn't even damaged. Peeled those notes right out of there like it weren't nothin'. Can you imagine if that was five hunnerd dollars US? *Disintegration*, dawg. Poverty and tears. But the day was saved by the Australian mint. Halle Berry, Hallelujah.

Oh, you in a hurry, is that it? Well, excuse me if you don't got time to listen to my very interestin' personal anecdote, dawg, but you in my house now an' you gots to play by the rules of the game. Five balls and stupendous prizes to be won, let's see how you do. Huh? Well, I don't give much of a flying fuck if you don't want to play, that's just how it's gotta be. I ain't handin' you over no blue koala less'n you at least makes out like there be some subterfuge here. You know the Five-O comes round here, right? Uh-huh, I seen 'em earlier, so when I makes delivery you best proceed off site with all due haste, motherfucker. Don't want you hangin' round here drawin' attention to my bidness, you feel me? Sure you do.

Now come on, homes, throw them balls in the air like you mean it. Oh ho ho, whattya know, first one straight in the hole, either that's beginner's luck or Australia gonna be callin' you up for the next Ashes, dawg. Try again. Ah, now don't be disappointed, the second one's always tricky. You throwin' too hard bra, don't know your own strength. An' the third one hits the rim! Damn, boy, you got game, wouldn't be surprised if you's at the next Olympics with this kinda form...Scratch that, number four was weak. You just got downgraded. No spot on the team for you. An' number five is mos def not alive, fact it ain't even close—no need to lose your temper, dawg, you still gets a prize.

Congratulations, sir, you get a cuddly toy of your choice, so long as it's blue and has Chlamydia. One koala for you, abuse it wisely, now get the fuck out of my sight and take a shower 'fore you come back next time, dawg. You smell like a retirement home.

One more fitty-dollar bill for the roll, thank you very much. That be three hundred already this mornin'. Damn, these hicks ain't exactly got what you might call a full social calendar. Nothin' to do all day but smoke it up an' watch *The View*. Still, keeps me busy I s'pose, an' it really could be worse. Fact is, I be better at sellin' crystal than anything else I ever done. Not that I done much.

Had me some punk-ass jobs in my day. Worked in a car park back in Freo for a couple months. That weren't bad, had me a golf buggy to drive round in for collectin' the tickets from the exit machines. Flipped the motherfucker when I took a corner too fast one time an' smashed into some rich asshole's Lexus. Boss was more concerned 'bout the car than me. Got fired for bein' reckless. Late-night shelf stackin' at Woolworths was safer, least in theory, but I lost that one too after I done accidentally sliced open a dozen two-litre bottles of Pepsi with a box cutter an' sprayed my supervisor in the face. Just 'bout everybody thought it was funny, 'cept for him.

Even tried answerin' phones in a call centre for Telstra but that was a motherfucking joke, man. They said I didn't make the grade 'cos I was spendin' too long bein' chatty with folks. Damn, bitches, an' you wonder why nobody likes you?

Gots me a clearer conscience dealin' meth. At least nobody gonna give me grief now Corporal Wallace got my back. Don't have to worry none 'bout gettin' rolled by small-time gangstas or addin' to my extensive collection of bruises or makin' sure I takes exactly seven minutes for my break. Just move the product an' multiply the moolah. 'Fore you know it, I'll be back in the good books an' maybe even have a little chedda put aside so's I can buy some studio time an' lay down some tracks, make a dope mixtape. Just gotta bide my time. Stay lower than a snake's belly. Don't die foolish.

Hey girls, I just know y'all is gonna brighten up my mornin' by winning not one, not two, but three fuzzy critters of your choice. Yes, that's right—it's real easy, just land three balls in one hole and you're a winner. I'll tell you what, since I'm in a good mood and you is by far, and I mean by a *looong* way, the most attractive ladies I seen all day, I'm gonna make it even easier for you. Land just two balls in any target and you will walk away with somethin' soft an' furry to stroke tonight. 'Less you single ladies already got similar plans.

No need to be embarrassed, girls, I myself am a confirmed bachelor. Now, who wants to cradle my balls in their palm? Just lean right over here and I will duly oblige.

5

Makin' so much paper the temperature of the earth just went up point zero zero zero one degrees. Corporal Wallace's roll be so large they musta cut down a fair chunk of Tasmania just to print all them pineapples. Chedda be rollin', dawg. S'got so I don't even see it as money no more. Just sticky yellow rectangles bundled into stacks of twenty—throw a laccy band round 'em and hand 'em over at the end of every night. Ben makes a note in his phone, weighs what product I got left to make sure I ain't skimmin', pats me on the back an' locks the door. S'like workin' at Maccy D's, 'cept I gots to bunk down next to the deep fryer.

Steph comes round later with some chow an' my medication but she don't want to chatter much. Seems she took a dislikin' to me after I snatched her Datch and besides, she's obvs part of the big man's business these days. Seen the light—or to be precise, smelt the money. She be all the way in now an' I's just an employee, an' a lowly one at that. No fraternising with the help, y'hear? A three-tier management structure, some shit like that. Can't say's I blame her for hatin' on me, an' she sure done hitched her cart to the right pony. That Corporal Wallace be a regular Phar Lap motherfucker.

The sheer extent of his operation is staggerin', dawg. He be runnin' nearly every small-time lab up the east coast an' that's usin' the dome, 'cos he ain't got no truck with importation. All them bikie gangs an' big-time Asian gangstas be tryin' to smuggle that shit in on container ships, hidden in fake antique furniture an' luxury cars an' up the puckered asshole of every Vaseline-totin' Bali-prison-bound motherfucker lookin' to make a fast buck. AFP so occupied searchin' the hold of every boat an' flashin' their Maglites up buttholes that they ain't got the time or the manpower to even begin investigatin' a fraction of the bush labs hereabouts. The game be wide open, for now at least, an' you gots to hand it to the big man, he done saw an opportunity an' swooped in there like a kookaburra snatchin' a big fat juicy mouse from its crib.

Only problem is consistency of the product. Ben got so many tweakers cookin' up for him that it ain't always what you might call top of the line, quality-wise. Some of that glass looks mighty rough to me, though I ain't no expert. Hold up, scratch that. What the fuck am I talkin' about? *Course*

I's an expert. I done become an expert these past few weeks. Don't have to smoke it or shoot it up to be able to tell when it ain't good shabu. Colour alone'll give that away. If that crystal be cloudy, there ain't no chance of meatballs, son. More'n likely that hit's gonna have a hard edge that will *fuck you up*. Sometimes it be more brittle than others too, like it'll just crumble in yo' fingers. Don't know if that's good or bad but it sure ain't the same chemical composition as the rock-hard glass that comes in other times.

Shit, it don't seem to matter none, not to the tweakers, not to the boss man. Could probs sell them ground-up stubbies an' they'd try an' smoke it, that's how fucken desperate some of these *28 Days Later* motherfuckers is. I can't even tell the diff no more between them all. This skinny-ass homeboy with a pinched face an' eyes like pissholes in the snow come round the other night, lookin' to score. You done smoked them two points already, son, I goes to him—bra, you gots to ease up on your intake. Motherfucker didn't have a clue what I was talkin' about. Thought he was the same hick I done sold to a couple nights earlier, in a different fucken town entirely. I swear he looked *exactly* the same, right down to his stained Kmart trackie dacks and Billabong tee. Motherfuckers must be gettin' their fashion advice from crankstyle dot blogspot dot com. Glass runway gettin' nasty this season.

Only thing keeps me from goin' insane in the membrane is watchin' them go through the charade of playin' Target Ball. Man, that is guaranteed chuckles. They's so feeble, they can hardly even throw five balls. Embarrassing, but I makes them do it anyway. Gots to keep up appearances, an' 'sides, it's the only kicks I got.

Worst part is nights. Ain't got no TV or music to listen to or nothin'. Time the show closes an' Ben collects the poke, it be past ten an' I got diddly squat to do 'cept bunk down on top the cuddly toys an' stare at the roof. Can't even go play cards with the other hands and I ain't allowed visitors. Been tryin' to work on some flow but the rhymes are dryin' up now that I's back on the meds. Denyin' me the one real pleasure I ever had an' the situation ain't about to change anytime soon. Now I's just stuck here, pissin' in a bucket in the corner, waitin' for the dawn to come.

Dawg, you gots to listen to reason over here, 'fore this turns into some kind of *Shawshank Redemption* situation. Some birds ain't meant to be caged, an' if I can't roam the halls of Hogwarts exchanging pleasantries with my fellow inmates an' breathin' some fresh fucken air into these lungs of mine, well, don't blame me if five years from now you finds a tunnel behind a poster of Nicki Minaj an' me paintin' the hull of some old boat three fucken thousand clicks from here, a'ight?

If you really wanted to, Mikey, you could bust out of here pretty easily.

You think I don't know that, bra?

So why don't you, then?

You know why, man.

Yeah, but I want to hear you say it.

'Cos I's part of the family now, a'ight? You happy? You an' Steph might as well be my moms and pops an' I be some teenager who got busted smokin' doobies on the garage roof, an' now I's grounded for a month. I am going out of my fucken mind cooped up in here, Ben.

An' I got caught short the other night an' had to take a dump in my piss bucket. That be humiliating, dawg. Ain't no need for that. You got me, a'ight? You got me, an' I'm workin' for you now an' I'm stayin' on the Kingdom an' that's it.

All this emptyin' my bucket in the mornin' while you stand over me is positively *medieval*, homes. This shit has got to be against the Geneva Convention, fo' sho. Gots me a mind to email the International Court of Human Rights an' word them up 'bout my case, you feel me?

What I'm concerned about is that restless-leg syndrome of yours.

Medical breakthrough, dawg. Wonders of science. I's all cured.

Well. Since you've been doing what you're told these past few weeks and there's not been any incidents, I suppose maybe I could allow you to leave the stall. With a strict perimeter. You're not to stray beyond the confines of the Kingdom.

Understood, boss. Message received loud and clear. Awesome, that's awesome. You won't regret it.

Don't make me.

So I can go an' do whatever I want?

Honestly, I don't really give a fuck anymore, Mikey. I'm

too busy to be worrying about you. Do what you fucken like, I don't care. You know there'll be consequences if you fuck up.

Mekong Delta *off the leash*. Now that's what I'm talkin' about. Breakin' out of this joint, goin' beyond these four walls, free at last even if Morgan Freeman an' his buddies all miss me, it don't matter, I's back on the road again with the wind in my locks. Well, in a manner of speakin'. The Kingdom ain't exactly the Pacific Ocean, but she'll have to do. Plenty to see an' do right here on the doorstep of Target Ball, after all.

Laydeez an' gentlemen, brothers an' sisters, friends an' enemies, may I reintroduce to you the prince of the rhymin' couplet, the host with the most, the ambassador of hip-hop bringin' his quip-pop to the land of the flip-flop, so raise yo' hands in the air an' jump, jump, 'cos Mikey Mekong Motherfucking Delta is back in da house.

A'ight, a'ight, *tranquilos mi hermanos*, let's take stock of my options here. First up, I needs me a major blow-out. All I gots to do to make that happen is procure me some hooch an' maybe some mooch, an' if I's lucky a little cooch. I can get my drank on sho' nuff, still gots me one or two peeps who'll front me the booze, ain't all unfriendly faces round these parts.

An' then there's the matter of a l'il taste of methamphetamine just to get me back on the road to perdition. Can't skim none from the main supply but alls I have to do is short-change a few of the tweakers. A shard here, a shard there and bam—I gots me just enough for a pipe, an' that's all I needs, baby. Can't be smokin' too much of that but a taste will fit the bill nicely an' get me where I wants to be.

After that, who knows, dawg? Maybe the laydeez will come flockin'. I still got game, an' extraordinary swag, plus the lines of interpersonal an' maybe even interspecies communication will be fully restored. My flow gonna be *scintillatin'*.

Open your mouth, Imma dive right in baby. Wrap that raspy tongue around my body till I slip down your throat. Head first, here I go, this be a fantastic voyage into the interior, all I needs is a rowboat an' a paddle to ride these rapids. Long journey ahead, Cap'n. S'gonna be a couple days 'fore we see light again, an' the way out ain't gonna be half as much fun as the way in. Can't never see the world from inside the skin of another, so this be as close as it gets, honey. Gonna pilot this vessel right through your arterial highways to get me a better look at how the other half lives. Left, right, left, two hundred and seventy degrees. These signposts are in a tawdry state of disrepair, girl. How's a sailor meant to find your visual cortex? I ain't no doctor of optometry. Here come the waves, each mightier than the last, an' we's surgin' upwards past the seas of tranquillity, serenity and fecundity, avoid that whirlpool leadin' to the lake of sorrow an' we's home free, adrift in your cornea an' starin' out through your windows on the world. Just me an' my little friends: torpedo number one, let's call him Tarantula, an' torpedo number two, let's call her Dame Helen Mirren. Master of the boat, stand by for launch and fire tubes one and two, they're in the water, they're away and brace for impact, brace, brace, brace.

Ba-ba-boom. I'm oozing out of you, baby. Slowly drippin' from your eyes, encased in a teardrop. Cry me a river and set me free. How 'bout a little poetry to mark the occasion? That's all hip-hop is, girl. The poetry of the ghetto. Whatchoo mean, Freo ain't no ghetto? I beg to differ. *Objection*, your honour. *Sustained*, counsellor, and yes, you may approach the bench whenever you damn well please. The only thing 'tween my 'hood an' chaos was the nine millimetre, or lack thereof. Think I'd of made it this far otherwise? All we had to battle with was blades, slicin' an' dicin', like samurai in miniature 'cept I was Ronin, a sword with no master. Fact I didn't even have me no sword, so what was I s'posed to do? Hang there till I got filleted? No ma'am, I got out, I got out, all the way to the eff bee eye, Clarice, but I still hear them lambs screamin'.

> *The silence of the orchestra*
> *between symphonic movements*
> *drowning the hiss of sidewinders*
> *is an agony upon which*
> *I have come to depend.*

See what I mean, girl? Take out the beat, turn down the bass an' all that's left is a dozen different versions of me vying for attention, all tryin' to snatch control of the lips an' tongue like I be a devil, like I needs to be exorcised—no, not exercised, can't you see the six-pack right there, girl I is ripped like Gosling, like Fassbender, like Butler in *300*. This is Sparta, right under my Dockers shirt.

What's the secret? What's the formula? Just grind up two tablets of Risperidone, whisk briskly in whisky until stiff, bake in the oven for half an hour an' then sprinkle four medium-sized shards of crystal methamphetamine on top. Lather in whipped cream. Cherry optional. Consume in entirety. Avoid driving, the use of heavy machinery and the Beatles' White Album. Side effects may include disorientation, unusually acute orientation, sexual dysfunction, sexual prowess, shyness, the need to talk to every motherfucker in the room, drowsiness, insomnia and the ability to listen to reggae without wanting to perforate your eardrums with a knitting needle.

A'ight, whoa there, horsey. Let's turn this down a notch for a second an' concentrate on what is real. That's the only way out this maze. What do you know for sure, dawg? Nothin'. A'ight, so let's throw this question open to our senses. What do you see, smell, taste, hear, touch, feel? Probs not reliable data, but it's all you got till you pop out the other side this motherfucker. All righty then, here goes.

Where am I? Look around, take it in. You are standing outside a trailer just behind sideshow alley. You appear to be peeking through a crack in a curtain hanging in the window of said trailer. The Hirsute Lady is inside, sitting on the edge of her bed, combing her legs.

What's that smell? Take a deep breath. Popcorn. Balloons. Mangoes.

Bad taste in the mouth? Lick those lips. Salty.

Did you hear that? The teeth of the comb sliding through individual hairs on her legs and back and face. A radio in the distance. A supernova.

Yes, but how do you feel deep inside, Mister Dempster? My apologies, Mister *Delta*.

Horny. Aroused. Deeply disappointed in my fellow man.

I see, I see. Well, in that case you had best proceed to the main event, and there are few cooches on this earth stranger than that which lies before you. Part the curtains, my good man. Tiptoe forward. Touch.

My, my, what big furry boobies you have, Mrs Wolf. May I comb them for you?

You certainly may, thin dark stranger. And what, might I ask, brings you to this neck of the woods?

I am but a wandering minstrel, m'lady, and perchance I paused in this quiet glade to gather my thoughts, which are legion, whereupon I glimpsed your fair furry form through yonder window.

You seek to soothe the savage beast that lurks within your breast?

I do, m'lady. Might I inquire as to your marital status?

I am betrothed. But my husband has gone forth and shall not return until he has had his fill of opossum.

I see. He, too, is a hairy gentleman of nocturnal appetites?

Not quite. The Leopard Man is his *nom de guerre*. Claws

and whiskers are his weapons. If we are to lie together, we must be swift. Should he return and discover us *in flagrante delicto*, it would not bode well for thee. Quickly, knave, remove thine Fremantle Dockers shirt. Do it slowly.

Oh, what unexpected delight to witness such musculature. Thou art ripped, much like Gerard Butler in that fine albeit overly stylised fillum *300*. Come to me, Spartan, come and forget what ails you between my firm thighs.

I see thou hast not waxed of late, m'lady, indeed perhaps not ever.

Alas, I am the ultimate challenge to and bane of the waxing industry. Does my hypertrichosis disturb thee? I notice thy phallus remains rigid. Prithee, let us not let the engorgement be wasted. Forge deeper into the forest, brave knight. Treasure lies within.

Ah yes, a few firm swipes of my sword should be sufficient to open a path through the hedgerow. Tell me m'lady, what team dost thou barrack for? Move a little to the left, please. And raise your buttocks just a tad—yes, that's it, verily.

Oh my. I should warn you, young studmuffin, that on occasion a great spout of female joy bursts forth from my lady parts, should you pleasure me just so. It can be an alarming emission for those unaccustomed to witnessing such eruptions. I shall give thee fair warning of its onset. You may want to take a few steps back and prepare thy shield.

Never fear, m'lady, I shall not baulk before thy pleasure fountain. Open thy floodgates and I shall add my own meagre five cubic centilitres of fluid to your gushing cascade.

Now, tell me, your preference of football team?

Oh. Oh. Hmm. *Sí, Antonio, dame tu chorizo*…I'm sorry, what? My sporting team? Why sir, you make a maiden blush asking such a personal question. Wait, let me get my leg up there—and the other one—oh yes, that's better. Umm, I suppose if pressed I would admit to a fondness for the West Coast Eagles.

Oh! That was an especially deep thrust. Has this illicit encounter just become a touch more thrilling for you, my lord?

Silence, wench. The Eagles, eh? I'll show you what the Dockers are going to do to you lot this year. Not literally, of course. We're not going to enter and ejaculate inside your bodies. That would be gay, and everyone knows one hundred per cent, no doubt whatsoever, that not a single footy player in the game today or in fact ever, anywhere, at any time likes to boff other dudes.

Uhh…what about the photos? I'm sure I saw photos of a knight with his squire's jousting pole in his mouth.

Mere horseplay. Good-natured banter. That doesn't count. Besides…

[ENTER, stage left, The Leopard Man, twirling his whiskers in a villainous manner. The fornicating couple is unaware of his presence.]

[ASIDE] And what have we here? Oh ho, that appears to be my wife with her legs over the shoulders of a strapping young lad. Despite his startling resemblance to a clean-shaven Gerard Butler, this will not do! I will step in at an opportune moment to bring this unholy rutting to a halt. I certainly shall. Any moment now. Hold on, just a second, I want to see this. Really? I didn't even know you could bend it that way. Oof, that looks painful but someone seems to be enjoying it. Wait, I recognise that expression. Here it comes. Shields up. Goggles on. And whoosh! Old Faithful's got nothing on that geyser. I should congratulate the boy on a job well done. But first, I'm going to kill him.

Oh husband, I did not hear you come in, being as I was otherwise occupied with this hunk o' spunk. Would you be so kind as to pass me a towel?

Didn't you put one down? Gah, woman, now I'll have to scrub the mattress again.

Hey there, Mr uh, Man. Is Leopard your middle name, or what? Please don't get the wrong idea—this is not what you think. I am but a wandering minstrel who, while passing, saw the lady in distress and rushed to her aid by removing a painful blockage from her cookie jar with an old family recipe of mine. The crisis has been averted! Chillax, dawg. Put yo' pearl-handled dagger away. That will not be necessary. Hey, watch what you're doin' with that, homie. You'll put some motherfucker's eye out. Hey. Hey!

Mikey. Hey. Get up—you can't sleep here.

Wha? Who dat? Where am I?

It's Leo. Brother, you're practically underneath the dumpster. How can you stand the smell? Does Ben know you're out here?

Uh yeah, he, uh, he cut the old apron strings. Gave me a set of training wheels.

Looks like you went a bit overboard. Haven't tied one on in a while, eh?

Naw, yeah, maybes got a bit carried away, huh? Help me up here, I seem to have fallen in some kinda hole. Thanks buddy. Hey, how's the, umm, missus?

She's good. Thick, lustrous coat, as always. I'm just heading in to comb her back. You want to come visit? Looks like you could do with a peppermint tea or something. Although it does kinda smell like you pissed yourself. Boy, when you let loose, you really don't hold back, do you? Go home and get cleaned up. It's one in the morning, Mikey. The party's over.

6

Mercury must be toppin' forty degrees an' still they be comin'. I knows they must be used to it an' all up here but damn, hot damn, this ain't no kind of way to live. Sideshow alley be packed full of folks in thongs, shorts an' singlets like they be at the beach. Didn't nobody in this state get the memo 'bout skin cancer? Slip, slop, slap, throw on a train driver's hat? I done seen more angry-lookin' moles today than at the Freo Centrelink. Get those unsightly blotches checked out, homegirls. An' put a lid on your fucken kid's dome. He's only five years old an' already he look like he been working in one of Gina's open-cast silver mines. Little fucker got a thousand-yard stare on him from squintin' 'gainst the sun all day. Clock of a thirty-year-old sniper on a child's body. Just ain't right.

Sweaty nut sacks an' titties a-go-go all up in here. Stink risin' off this crowd like someone done pissed on a dead fox. Can practically smell the Chlamydia. Four chickadees already slipped me their numbers an' it ain't even lunchtime yet. Sad thing is, I threw 'em all away. Cray, huh? Here's me with a head full of fucked-up fantasies, desperate to bust a nut, an' I still wouldn't slip my bookmark in none of these local cookbooks. Man, I wouldn't even turn down the corner of a page. Ain't exactly brimmin' with hotties round here though there was one with a nice rack come through earlier. I'd motorboat her titties, but that's about my limit, dawg.

Been so busy I ain't even had time to drain the lizard but it don't matter none anyways. Think I done sweated out all the fluids in my body, probs couldn't squeeze out three drops of piss. Target Ball stand be pumpin' even though it's like a fucken microwave oven in here an' my shorts is so soaked with sweat they's turned a different colour. My damp appearance don't seem to be particularly off-puttin' to the local populace, though. They loves the cheap games, an' mine is 'bout the cheapest on the alley.

Actually might make more chedda on the hoops than slingin' crystal today, though it only takes a couple of buys to seriously boost the poke. Too much like hard work, all this arguin' with sunburnt motherfuckers who think they been screwed by the game. Which they have, but I ain't about to tell them that, dumb fucken clems. Angry, scrunched-up clocks, fat bellies, muffin tops and kids with sauce and ice-cream smeared all over their chins. An endless fucken procession of whingein', dribblin' mediocrity. Sugar, the big fucken pine-apple and K-Rudd. This is Nambour. Welcome to Queensland. Still, ain't no diff really to the other side of the border.

Just when I's gettin' comfortable with my prejudices 'gainst the wrinkled squinters, thar she blows, waitin' patiently in the queue for her turn. Pretty obvious she ain't linin' up to win no giraffe for the kiddlywinks. Cheeks pinched an' lips thin, hair pulled back tight in a ponytail so's I can see every crease on her forehead. Eyes flittin' 'tween me an' the crowd, watchin' for Five-O.

My guts do a back flip an' nail the landin' so sweet the judges are holding up scores worthy of gold. Fuck a duck, it's her. Some good Samaritan musta taken her in that night in Mudgee, fixed her up an' pulled her out the mess I done left her in, but she don't look so good now. Hit the glass highway, looks like.

Ay carumba. What'm I gonna do here? What if she makes a scene, blows the game wide open? An' why she comin' to score in the middle of the day, right in front of all these clueless clems? How'm I gonna justify handin' out a blue koala when all an' fucken sundry can see exactly what's goin' on? Maybes I'll tell her to come back later, or see me on my break, pretend she's an old flame or somethin', which she is, kinda. I seen her cooch anyways, s'pose that counts.

Wait up, dawg. False alarm. It ain't her. Nah, it's just some other chick who been suckin' the pipe a l'il too much lately. Damn, I coulda sworn. Fell for that ol' chestnut again,

Mikey. Basic rule of crank dealin' one-o-one—no matter what the tweakers look like when they gets started, even if they is Brad Pitt or Angelina Jolie-resemblin' motherfuckers, couple months shootin' up shards an' they all looks like Steve fucken Buscemi. No offence to the guy, he's a great fucken actor an' all, but you don't wanna be imaginin' the motherfucker all trussed up in leather thongs like the Pittster in *Troy*, do ya?

Hang back, girl. That's right, stand over there till I gets rid of these chump jerkwads.

Yo, takin' fifteen for lunch over here, people, so I'm closin' up after this gentleman completes his turn. Yeah, I'm real sorry 'bout that, missus, but I ain't got nobody to relieve me over here, an' I is in sore need of some relief, you feel me? Less'n you wanna spot me? Naw, that's what I thought. Come back a l'il later, darlin', I'll give you five balls for free, straight up.

Okay then, sir, how'd you go there? Two from five ain't bad now, most folks strike out quicker'n that. This half pint your daughter? Alakazam there, honey. Yup, that's what us carnies say to one another 'stead of hello. S'like the magic words, you know? She's a cutie, ain't she?

Tell you what, buddy, since you been the only customer ain't shouted at me in the last ten minutes an' not accused me of cheatin', here's a genuine unicorn for the little one. You like that, honey? See how he's got a magical horn comin' out his head? You keep your eyes open if you's ever in the forest, an' maybes you'll spy one fo' reals. Hey, no problem, brother, it's my pleasure just to see the little un smilin'. You take care now an' have a good day here on the Kingdom. Watch your heads, I gots to lower this shutter.

As for you, miss, come on round the side here an' I'll let you in.

Damn, girl, what's the dally-o comin' round lookin' to score in front of all the families an' shit? You gots to be more discreet than that.

Sorry...It's just, I heard you was holdin' an' I really need a fucken hit, you know?

A'ight, a'ight, cool your jets, it's all good, girl—I got your six. Just a point you be after?

Fucken oath. Thing is, though, I've only got forty but I thought maybe you could help me out, mate.

Seriously? This ain't no soup kitchen, girl. Who told you I might cut you a deal?

Nobody. I just thought, you know, the show's in town for a couple of days, I'll sort you out next time. C'mon, mate, I'm good for it, I promise.

First up, quit callin' me 'mate'. I ain't your friend, an' no use pretendin' otherwise, a'ight? Secondly, why should I do you a solid? I ain't never seen you before, girl.

All right, look, fuck, what's it gonna take? God, please don't be weird.

That is not how I roll, sweet cheeks. Throw that shit right the fuck out yo' head, an' Christ, what the fuck's wrong with you anyways, offerin' up your cooch for crank? Ain't you got no self-respect left at all? Aw now, don't be cryin',

Jesus—look, let's sit down for a minute, huh? There you go. Dry them tears an' don't be worryin'. I'll give you a fucken point for forty even though my boss would bust my balls if he knew I done it, so this is just 'tween you an' me, a'ight? An' don't be thinkin' it was the waterworks done it, neither. I'm lettin' you off here 'cos you reminds me of someone I knew a little while ago.

And it ain't my place to say this, but I'm gonna go right ahead in case you gots nobody else tellin' you but, girl, you needs to kick, you hear me? Kick while you still gots your teeth. Lemme see that face. Damn, I bet all the boys asked you to the formal, huh? Yeah, it ain't too late, you know? It ain't never too late.

Damn near broke my heart seein' that messed up tweaker chick. Maybe it's 'cos she come round when she did in the day an' maybe it's 'cos she was the spittin' image of Deb from Mudgee an' maybe it's 'cos this whole dirty fucken scenario is weighin' on my shoulders but whatevs, all I can think of is gettin' out. Must be cray even considerin' it after what Ben done told me would happen if I didn't stay put but I's backed into a corner here an' there's just got to be a way, right?

I kept my nose clean long 'nuff for him to let his guard down a little, an' the way business is goin' he be rakin' in so much paper he's got his hands full jugglin' what to do with it. Tricky thing 'bout the proceeds of crime—whatcha gonna do with all the cold hard chedda? Can't keep frontin' up to no bank with pocketfuls of cash, ten grand at a time. They's only gonna get suspicious an' call the Five-O or the ATO. Fucken unpaid tax. That's how they brings down all the greats—Al Capone, Wesley Snipes, Paul Hogan.

Demand for ice is practically outstrippin' supply. Some days I's runnin' real low an' Ben has to make some furious fucken calls to secure me a re-up. Some toy manufacturer in China probs had to hire an extra dozen street urchins just to sew up all the additional blue koalas we ordered. Yup, we's a regular cottage industry over here on Target Ball, keepin' 'bout a hunnerd Aussie meth workers in jobs, 'scuse me, workin' meth *families* is I believe the correct expression, not to mention the thirty-five cents a day we is lavishin' on our junior employees in the People's Republic.

Fact is, Ben ain't been around much lately. Seems to me he must have a couple of big labs out bush round here somewheres. Plenty of quiet spots in the hinterland where you could stink the place up an' nobody'd bat an eyelid. Obviously he's off takin' care of bidness, an' if it weren't for his lap cat Steph hangin' round tryin' to act like she a gangsta's moll now or somethin', I'd be all on my ownsome. They ain't got the personnel to man the size of operation they got now, an' I figure that means I got two options. Either I goes to Ben an' demands a promotion, or I gets the fuck out of Dodge 'fore Wyatt Earp an' his posse of lawmen come ridin' through. Don't want my clock on no wanted poster, dawg.

It's a risk, though, a major fucken risk. I wanna keep my legs, you feel me? I'd have to avoid the roads. Ain't like they's leavin' their keys lyin' around no more anyways. Nah, better to get kitted up an' go bush, head inland to Maleny or Woodford, maybes hide out on some hippie property for a couple of weeks or set up camp in the forest for a while until the Kingdom moves upstate. Then I could skip back on down to one of those small airports on the coast an' buy me a ticket out of the hot zone. Virgin Blue down to Radelaide, where they ain't never gonna find me. Shit, that's a decent plan. All I needs is some chedda to see me through an' that's it, motherfucker. I be walkin' right on out this joint. Can't take too much though. Don't wanna make Bruce Banner all green an' angry.

Tonight. S'gotta be tonight. Ben's away, Steph ain't got the game, everybody on the Kingdom be straight-up exhausted—seemed like just about the busiest day of the season so far. Ain't nobody gonna pay much attention to my exact where-abouts. Plus, lookee what I gots right here. Just counted the poke an' I moved almost two g's worth of glass today, plus rolled eight hunnerd buckeroos of legit paper on the hoops.

A'ight, Mikey, here's what you do. Hand the two large to Steph an' tell her you're keepin' the rest to bankroll tomor-row's games. That way she'll call Ben with the report an' then hit the hay, probs tell me to go enjoy myself after a job well done. Pat on the back an' all that shit. Gold fucken star. Lock up the stand an' head west, for the forest, 'cross them paddocks. Reckon I can cover ten, maybe fifteen ks 'fore dawn.

Steph probs won't even notice I is gone till the stand don't open at eleven. That gives me a full twelve-hour start, an' then by the time she asks around an' calls Corporal Wallace, I'll just be 'nother phantom in the woods. Won't exactly be home free, but as good as, brother. They ain't gonna go to all the trouble of launchin' no manhunt, not this time, not for little ol' Mikey Dempster an' his eight hunnerd. I be gone. Disappeared.

In the wind, motherfuckers.

I think there's three of 'em back there somewheres. Ben an' two others, but I can't be sure. They ain't real close but they's a lot closer than I'd like. Fuck me, how'd this happen? Shut up, Mikey, shut up, you dumb prick, you know exactly how this happened. No, I don't, that's a lie, a cruel hurtful lie, I do not know *exactly* how this happened, no need to exaggerate an' make this worse, dawg. I's in enough trouble already over here. Yes, a'ight, I admit, I got an idea *roughly* how this happened—are you happy now? I's not aware of the finer points of the morning's events, how could I be? Well, someone must have seen you, asshole. Someone must have seen you leaving last night. Well, duh, I know that now, a'ight? It's totally fucken obvious. Who, though? Who seen you? You was real careful none of the hands noticed you leavin', an' Steph was already in bed. Her eyelids was droopin' while she was talkin' to you so it weren't likely her now, was it? Well, I don't know then, do I? You know as much as I do.

Probs one of the tweakers. Yeah, that'd be who it was.

One of those motherfucking crankheads musta come round again this mornin' lookin' for an early score an' maybes seen me flittin' out last night an' fessed up to Steph or Ben 'cos word was they was lookin' for me. Holy fuck, I hope it weren't that girl I done helped out yesterday. Biatch, do not tell me you sold me out for a point. She probs did, man. She probs did. Wouldn't put it past her. Did you see the look in her eyes when you gave her that point for forty? Like a fucken kid openin' his Xbox on Christmas mornin'. No question she would of sold you down the river, no doubt about it, you dumb-ass motherfucker. What the fuck you thinkin', helpin' her out like that? You know these tweaks'll trade you up for glass in a fucken heartbeat—shit, dawg, ain't you ever gonna learn not to show no moments of weakness?

An' now look at the mess you're in, dickhead. All cut up an' bleedin' from crashin' through the bush like a wild animal, dog tired from not hardly gettin' no sleep an' you even done tore yo' Dockers shirt. Right down the fucken seam at the side. Look at that shit, y'all is a disgrace to the club, boy.

Never mind that, fuck sake, never mind yo' damn Fremantle Dockers, they ain't gonna save you now. Matthew Pavlich ain't gonna swing down out no tree dressed in a fucken loincloth to protect you from the great white hunters. You is on your own, dawg. Keep movin'. They's still a ways behind you, an' they ain't movin' fast 'cos they don't know where you is at, not yet anyways, so don't be makin' no dick moves to tip 'em off neither. Just stay on this old critter trail an' don't stop, you know it's gonna lead to water eventually an' then maybes you can jump off a cliff into the river like in the movies an' get washed downstream.

How come they's always jumpin' off cliffs an' bridges an' shit in movies, usually with a fireball behind 'em, an' they never gets hurt or nothin' when they hits the water, like three hunnerd feet below or whatever? You'd think at least there'd be a couple of broken legs or somethin' but nah, they always bobs back up, shakes their hair an' proceeds to the next scene like it weren't nothin'. Gonna boycott me any movie from now on that's got a fallin' into water from great height scene, that shit be stale, dawg.

Yo, any chance of you concentratin' on the matter at hand, motherfucker? Case you forgot, you is bein' pursued through the forest by what is quite possibly your angry boss an' a couple of bikies with shotties. Might wanna focus up here, homeboy. Try an' filter the choir in yo' head down to just the lead singer, you feel me? A'ight, that's the straight-up dope right there, all you cats step the fuck off, I needs to keep this real. There you go. Quieten down now, boys. This ain't the time for idle chatter. Phase out. Drop the snare, the bass, the string section, lead guitar, back-up singers and ahh, there it is. Just a low hum.

Sometimes you just gots to laugh, right? This ol' wombat trail don't lead to no ragin' torrent. It's just a creek, dirty an' stinkin', hardly even a trickle. Still, don't know if they got a bloodhound or whatever but maybes if I wade upstream I can throw 'em off the scent. That's what a fugitive's s'posed to do, right? Fuck it, I'll give it a go, gots to be worth a try an' least I ain't leavin' no footprints on the trail.

Christ all fucken mighty I damn near split my dome open on that fucken rock. It's slippery as fuck all up in this biatch. Now I's soaked along with everythin' else. This ain't no good, I's gettin' out of here an' back on the trail though hold up, hold up, what's that up there? The edge of a property, maybes? Lemme just crawl up this bank here an' see what I can eyeball. Well, that is a weird sight but whatever, I don't care, it looks like good cover to me an' maybes there's a road on the other side...shit, bad case of déjà vu. I been here before, 'cept this time I ain't got the cover of darkness.

Pineapples. Thousands an' thousands of pineapples, all in rows, stretchin' as far as the eyeball can see. Well, shit. I always thought they grew on trees an' had to be knocked from the branches like coconuts. Apparently not, genius. They grow right out the *ground*. Damn. S'like a footy pitch covered in spiky yellow balls ready to be punted. Better get a hoof on 'fore these motherfuckers burst out the woods behind me. Pick a row, any row. Start runnin', Mikey, think I hear someone comin'.

Damn, I knew all that bein' closed up in the stall would affect my fitness. I's close to beat now, don't think my legs got much more in 'em. Keep goin', dawg, just keep goin'. You still got a jump on them that's followin' you. An hey, there's a car, over there at the edge of the field. Maybes it's the owner of this here place. Maybes I can seek refuge or hide or somethin'. Fucken pineapples, they's all around me an' I can't see straight no more, 'cept here's a clearin' an' the driver of that car musta seen me 'cos here he comes, skiddin' up an' covered in dust, 'cept it ain't no car, it's a ute aww, no, it can't be, can it?

They flushed me out into this here pineapple crop an' now I'm done, I can't go no further, I's exhausted. Can't believe they come after me so quick an' hard, I didn't do anythin' so bad, though, did I? Just snuck off for a little explorin', went walkabout for the night. Ben ain't gonna punish me too hard.

Maybes just a hidin' an' then I's back to square one on Target Ball until a better opportunity to flee comes up 'cos, you know, you gots to see I can't stay there the rest of my days, I wanna be free man, I want out. I's just a kid from Freo, dawg, just let me go, will ya? Please, for fuck sake, I's beggin' you to let me go.

Wait. Oh my God. You're not gonna…Let go of me, motherfuckers. Don't. Ben, please, I know we been here before but don't do this, it's barbaric, it's what they did to slaves an' that's my kickin' foot, my foot and oh, look at all them pineapples all in their rows so pretty an' strange an' unexpected. I never knew.

7

I see them lookin' with their beady, greedy eyes. I'm one of them now, they's sayin'. Part of the freak show. Peg leg. Gimpoid. Quasi-fucken-modo. Ain't got me no hump or no little hands or hair all over my face like some round here but I s'pose the whispers don't lie. I truly is part of the family now. Least he didn't take to me with no axe. Probs would of died if he had, bled out in the dirt with all them pineapples. Won't never be able to eat that fruit no more, not without rememberin'—though to be honest, I don't remember much.

Woke up in the hospital with some rough-as-guts mother-fucker I'd never clocked before sittin' by my bedside, keepin' guard sort of thing. Official story was I'd had an accident on the show, got my ankle crushed in one of the rides. No mention of a psychotic former soldier wielding a club hammer from Bunnings.

Kept me on the ward a couple days 'fore they sent me back to the Kingdom on a crutch. Nervous-lookin' doc said I'd have to keep the cast on for a month, maybe more, but even then the bone would never knit anythin' like it was before. I'd have a limp the rest of my days an' wouldn't be runnin' the hunnerd metres for Straya after all. An' he didn't think I'd ever be able to wear sneakers again. Not enough support, he says. Too painful if I rolled the ankle. Dumb motherfucker obv ain't never heard of hi-tops. Plenty of choice out there for b-ballers an' limpin' cripples like myself. Gonna hit me up Rebel Sport soon as I crack this plaster biatch open.

Music career be on hold for the time bein', I guess, probs TV show pitches too. Doc said I had to be religious with the meds, so there goes my flow. Hepped up on painkillers now, so I's gettin' weird dreams an' I can't really think straight most of the time. Pretty zonked, for reals. Just 'bout all I can handle is sittin' here in Target Ball, makin' up stories 'bout what happened to my foot when the clems ask, takin' their money an' not even botherin' with no ballyhoo to draw 'em in. Tweakers come round as always, a steady stream of balding, toothless assholes seekin' the legendary blue koala. Everyone's a winner, ain't that the truth.

Been like that for a week or two now, kinda lost track if I's truthful. Ain't no real artifice to it no more, neither. Everybody on the Kingdom knows what sort of business goes down here. They turns a blind eye. Most of 'em just ignore me. They don't want to get involved, an' I don't blame 'em. Once in a while someone comes round though, to say alakazam an' maybe bring me a coffee or a sandwich so's they don't have to watch me strugglin' down the alley on my crutch, a reminder to everyone on the show 'bout the price of admission. Ain't even worth statin' what the penalty'd be next time I stray. Not that I could anyways. Be months afore I can walk unassisted an' the doc says I may not be able to drive again without some pain, so I's stayin' put an' everybody knows it, Ben most of all.

Runnin' the blue-koala line without hardly any interference at all now. Tally up the poke at the end of the night an' hand it over, get my re-up in the mornin' and repeat. Now that I's hobbled, Ben trusts me to get the job done. Well, it ain't strictly that he trusts me, more that he knows he owns me, mind, body an' soul. Sad, ain't it? How the mighty Mekong Delta has fallen. Can't really go much lower neither. Course, if there's a way, I'll probs find it. I ain't nothin' if not reliable in that there department.

Kingdom been all over the joint since Nambour. Flittin' around the state, settin' up here an' there, fillin' showgrounds an' bringin' entertainment to the sweaty QLD masses. S'been all a blur to me. I's back to sleepin' on a camp bed in the stall an' pissin' in a bucket in the corner. Can't really roam much further.

Amazin' what you can get used to, though. Tried to do me a full tour of the showgrounds here in Toowoomba yesterday mornin' 'fore we opened for business. Don't want the one good leg I gots left to waste away. S'weird, I kinda got more friends on the show now than I ever did before. Probs they just feels sorry for my ass.

Got me a few tips from Boris the strongman. Most I ever spoke to the dude. He dropped the Russian super-soldier experiment act an' showed me a weights routine to help my rehabilitation. Gotta build my upper-body strength, he reckons, take the weight off that foot. Sho' nuff that's some good advice, an' I sure 'preciated him bein' straight with me. He even gave me a couple small dumbbells so's I can do curls while I'm sittin' round in the stall sweatin' my ass off all day.

My diet been healthier too since the, uh, *accident*. Delia from Shark Bites been bringin' me soup an' the odd stir fry. Makes a change from all the deep-fried shit I been wolfin' these past months an' I's feelin' a little less zonked every day. I suppose this is what the clems call normal. 'Bout as close to it as I gets, anyways.

Still, it don't raise the spirits much visitin' with the old carnies that been on the Kingdom most of their lives. Boris got hounded out of the bodybuilder circuit 'cos he was queer, an' he got that sadness on his clock for all to see. Then there's Voltan, what calls hisself the Master of Electricity. Old coot wears a purple leotard with a V cut out the chest. Grey hairs stickin' out the gap match the eyebrows standin' ninety degrees out from his face 'cos of all the shocks he took to the dome. Also, motherfucker wears a *cape*, an' no shoes. He be carryin' some sad story too, 'bout a wife an' daughter got burned up in the bushfires years back.

The Doc's another one like him. Gotta be 'bout eighty years old an' still ridin' the Wall of Death on his old Norton, pet ferret stickin' out his pants. Word is once that little critter buys the farm the Doc's gonna fuck up one of his stunts on purpose an' go out in a ball of fire. Way things are goin' I'll probs be still here when it happens, the oldest fucken ice dealer in town.

Suppose that's my future, right there in them dusty trailers. If I don't do time for slingin' meth, I'll end up as some eccentric old coot with a novelty act, a flea circus maybes, or offerin' to put the clems in touch with dead relatives. Step right up, folks, come see the man who's been slingin' ice since before you were a twinkle in yo' momma's eye. Mekong Delta, medium and spirit guide, off his clock with meds an' madness, limpin' around the Kingdom sometime in the year twenty thirty-four, not even able to remember how I got there. A crystal casualty, a relic, spoutin' some arcane hip-hop flow from the days of yore. Roll up, roll up, laydeez an' gentlemen, my swag be trill, fo' shiz, an' that's the triple truth.

Yo, this must be her now, boss. Shit, you can't really mistake that growl, huh?

I warned her about Fords, but she wouldn't listen.

Oh, come on, you got to admit that's a classic. What year is it—sixty-seven?

Sixty-four. Fuck knows how many times it's been rebuilt.

Don't matter though, right? S'just a show car. Ain't like she's gonna race it or nothin'.

What's the betting something goes wrong with it within, say, six weeks?

You's the expert, boss. I just like how it sounds. *Mus-tang.* Pretty dope, though I can't say much for the colour. What is that, yellow? Orange? Kinda makes my eyeballs bleed.

You'll get no arguments from me. She wanted pink, but I couldn't find one. The good news is, the Datsun's yours now. Funny how that worked out.

'Preciate that, dawg, but the docs say I can't drive.

Isn't that cast due to come off soon?

Couple more days, they said. Yo, is it Steph's birthday or somethin'? Thought she was a Virgo.

Yeah, nah, it's just a perk. Too much cash building up, she said we had to get rid of some.

Hey, if you's handin' out gifts, I always fancied me a jet ski.

What the fuck would you do with a jet ski, Mikey?

Travel round Australia. Y'know, in the water, like.

Yeah, I got that. For why?

Dunno. Just to see the coastline from a different perspective. Can't be many guys done it.

Uh-huh. And when were you planning on doing this?

Yeah, about that. Don't suppose this job comes with twenty days' annual leave?

Nah, and there's no fucken super, right.

What about when we're up north this winter? Couldn't

I take a couple of weeks off then, go see my moms?

We'll see. Don't get your hopes up.

Shit, look at them crowdin' round her. I'd be worried 'bout all the attention a ride like that attracts, I was you.

Like I never thought of that.

An' if you don't mind me sayin', has Steph put on weight? She be lookin' a little, uhh, what's a polite way of puttin' this—a little more voluptuous?

What's that supposed to mean?

A'ight, don't get your back up, I's just sayin' she looks a little rotund to me. She been hitting the fried dimmies pretty hard of late, or what?

What fucken business is it of yours if she has?

None. None of my beeswax. Forget I said it. Let's move on to the next topic 'fore I ain't got no legs left to stand on.

This may come as a surprise, but I'm probably going to have to promote you.

Fo' reals? Wait, don't tell me. Regional sales manager, right? You want me to hit the road an' hawk the product, drum up some new custom, go cold callin'.

That's about it, actually.

Bullshit.

It's basically what you were doing anyway after you stole Steph's car that time. Going through small towns, talking to locals, creating demand.

Yeah, but that was different, homes. I was on the lam an' just tryin' to offload my supply, turn a quick buck.

I'm about to lay my hands on a considerable amount of

crystal and I want to move it as quickly as possible. You can help me with that.

S'pose I could, but seriously? You'd trust me to do that after all the, uh, misunderstandings 'tween us?

Oh, I wouldn't send you out alone, Mikey. I know you'd never come back. You'd have a partner, someone with explicit instructions for how to proceed in the event of you doing another fucken runner. Or should I say stumble.

No need to rub my nose in it. An' when would this wonderful rural adventure begin?

This winter.

What about my holidays?

I said not to get your hopes up about that.

Yeah, yeah, thanks a fucken bunch. It sounds just dandy, drivin' round Queensland with some dirty fucken greaser as my conjoined twin, gettin' teens hooked on ice.

Thug life. Isn't that what you always wanted?

Didn't figure it would be quite so glamorous.

Quit whining. You could've died several times already this year. You want today's re-up or not?

Sure thing, but look, why don't you go for a spin with the lady of the house first, see if y'all can overcome your prejudice concernin' the Ford Motor Company. Maybes once you is behind the wheel you'll be converted by the convertible, you feel me? I can hold the fort here. I got your six.

And you won't do anything stupid while I'm gone, no dumb moves?

Scout's honour...Yo, Steph, ride be trill, girl. Props. I's

just tellin' your nearest an' dearest here that you two love-birds oughta head on out for a romantic drive round the hills or somethin'.

It's getting this one into the passenger seat of a Ford that's the problem.

Nah, look, I'll go with you. Just let me bring some tools, so we're prepared for the inevitable.

Really? You want to take her out?

So long as I don't have to drive.

Oh don't worry, nobody's driving this but me.

Glass House Mountains ain't far. Heard there's a good lookout, an' it is a weekday so maybes you two'll find a nice private spot for some *sweeeet lo-vin' action*, knowhumsayin'?

Are we leaving this in charge?

I was thinking about it.

Do we trust it now?

No, but he's not going anywhere. The alternator on the Datsun's still fucked and it's a long walk to Brisbane.

Even longer with a limp. All right, let's go before we get caught up with something.

Remember what I said, Mikey. No fucking around.

Five by five, you is in the pipe. Y'all have a good time now, y'hear?

That's right, motherfucker, you take off for a drive in your girlfriend's fancy ride an' hope nobody from Five-O's got eyes on you, dawg. A fun day out for all the family—nothin' to see here, officers, just a couple o' small-time carnies with so much chedda they's rollin' in a pristine vintage Mustang that musta cost thirty grand.

An' did you clock that bling around Steph's neck? Damn, least someone been enjoyin' the fruits of my labours but it probs ain't too smart advertisin' her newfound wealth like that, am I right? Woman be hatin' on me ever since I snatched the Datch an' I wouldn't be the faintest bit surprised if it was her sicced the dogs on me an' told 'em to bring me back minus one foot. She been warmin' to the bidness like a brown snake out sunbathin' on the bitumen. Ben be the power playa but Steph, well, she fast becomin' the numbers operator. Got it all totted up on her fucken MacBook, spreadsheets an' everything. God damn Excel witch, that one, keepin' the accounts nice an' clean. Ain't five cents don't go unaccounted for.

Worst part of it is, she don't even refer to me by name. Fact she can't even bring herself to say 'him' or 'the kid' or 'asshole' or nothin'. Just calls me *it* or *this* with a look on her face like she done just stepped in somethin' real unpleasant. How much did *it* make today? What time is *it* opening the stall? *It* puts the fucken lotion in the basket. I's just some Gollum-type motherfucker to her an' that's why I gots to keep sweet with Corporal Wallace, Shabu Division. Seems he's the lesser of two weevils.

Least I got the day to myself for a change. Kingdom ain't open till tonight an' less'n any tweakers comes lookin' to score I's free to enjoy the sights and sounds of glorious outer Toowoomba. Be still my beatin' heart. Not exactly in the best shape for strollin' round the shops seekin' bargains an' I don't got no chedda anyways. Steph's got me on a choke chain far as that goes. Tugs it every night till I coughs up every dollar of what I made, slingin' crystal and throwin' hoops. Ain't got five bucks to my name. All's I can do is go lookin' for teenagers an' try to scrounge a ciggie from them, maybes a hit from a Slurpee if I's lucky.

Way them clouds is formin' today I doubt they'll be gone long anyways. Ben's probs thinkin' he'll get some action for agreein' to ride in her tan Mustang, damn if it don't look the colour of diarrhoea, not that I'd ever say nothin'. If it was me an' my girl I'd find us one of those dirt roads leadin' off into the forest, park under a tree in the shade and break out the blanket, spread that mofo out on the grass down by a quiet little creek. Kinda honey I'd be with'd probs strip down to her skin right there, knowin' there was nobody around an' not givin' much of a fuck anyways if there was.

Maybes we'd wade into the creek an' get shocked by how cold the water was on our asses when we sat down. Come out shiverin' even though it be thirty somethin' degrees an' throw ourselves down on that blanket to let the sun dry us off. She'd get me to rub sunscreen into her back then an' hup the ass would go in the air all ready an' willin' an' waitin' for me to do what I gots to do.

Maybes a couple wallabies would come out the trees while we was doin' it an' turn their heads sideways to watch. That would make us laugh an' she'd turn around then so I got the full-frontal effect. Man, I'd Yogi Bear that pic-a-nic

211

basket. We'd just be workin' up a sweat when it'd start to rain but that wouldn't stop us, just the two of us out there in the wild like animals, like...hold up, whisky tango foxtrot motherfucker, I just felt drops. Yeah, here it comes, fo' reals. Here comes the deluge.

8

The Kingdom be eerie now there ain't hardly nobody left. Twelve hours of constant stingin' rain. Been a cray night, hardly got no sleep 'cos I was stumblin' around in the dark like everybody else, tryin' to protect what rides we could from the water 'fore all the hands done cleared out. The Ferris wheel an' carousel ain't never seen so much rain an' they is already old, so if the damp gets in it's curtains. Corrosion, you feel me? Maybes we don't notice it straightaway but next summer when there's a dozen kiddies on the big wheel an' one of the struts snaps an' the whole thing comes tumblin' down? Fucken nightmare. We'd all be out of a job, not to mention havin' the blood of some maimed half pints on our hands.

Weren't no time to dismantle the big rides, so they's

gettin' left behind till all this blows over. Plenty of places to hole up, though, an' wait for my chance. Ben an' Steph took off an hour ago, didn't even notice me lurkin' behind. 'Spose they thought I'd hitch a ride with somebody else, that I wouldn't have the balls to run again. Been hidin' out in one of the portaloos ever since, tryin' to formulate a plan. Fucken stinks in here.

Or maybe it's just me. Not exactly dressed for inclement weather. This old Dockers shirt seen better days. Stuck with me, though. Been tore up the side, sewed back together, had my blood on it more times than I can count, souvlaki an' sauce stains come and gone—yessiree, you gots to hand it to Freo, we don't never quit even if the rain is lashin' down an' we is tired an' beat an' carryin' a bad injury. Still got somethin' left in the tank, enough for one last foray forward to try an' kick the winning goal.

Made me an executive decision to crack open that plaster cast on my foot 'cos it was slowin' me down so bad. Probs too early but the damn thing was gettin' in the way. Foot didn't look that bad when I saw it. Still swole an' black-lookin', but at least I was able to give it a good old scratchin' an' a wash. Wrapped 'er up in a clean bandage an' even managed to get one of my Nikes on, though I had to make some alterations that damn near broke my heart. Cut the heel section out completely so I's wearin' it kinda like a slip-on. Ain't gonna win no design award but leastways I can walk normal, in a manner of speakin'. Still got the crutch to keep the weight off it, but I do feel relieved seein' it out that fucken plaster.

Rain be poundin' down real hard now on the roof of my less-than-salubrious temporary accommodations. Can't hardly hear myself think all up in here. Needs me a bit of luck, but surely I must be due my annual quota. Ain't caught a break all summer. Just gotta wait it out here for a bit longer till I'm in the clear, then hoof it.

S'all quiet out there, seems, 'cept for the rain. Don't sound like it's easin' off much. Maybe I should crack this biatch open an' have a look-see. Real slow now, never know who's watchin'.

Jesus, there sure is a lot of water on the ground. Basically sittin' in the middle of a river of mud here. Best be careful with my fucked-up foot. Don't want to be coppin' no infections.

A'ight, c'mon then, Mikey, get yo' ass out there, son, let's bounce. Clouds be dark overhead. All's left is just me an' some old run-down machines, an' that one carousel horse whose cover got blown off, givin' me the evil eye.

This crutch sure is comin' in handy for testin' how deep the mud be. Shit, can't hardly see nothin' through this curtain of water pourin' off my cap. Ain't exactly planned this too good, homes. Which way am I gonna go? Maybes if I head out past the showgrounds an' keep walkin' I'll get picked up by some good Samaritan goin' in the opposite fucken direction to Ipswich an' everyone else on this freak show. Bound to be somebody who'll take pity on a poor ol' boy with a crutch, right?

Hold up. Stop for a second there, bra. Coulda sworn

THE GLASS KINGDOM

someone was callin' my name. Must be the meds, 'cos ain't
nobody here 'cept me an'…there it is again. No mistakin' it
that time. Naw, it can't be. He wouldn't come back in this,
not for me. He don't care that much, right?

Wrong. Wrong, wrong, wrong. It's Corporal Benjamin
Wallace an' he sounds pissed. Hide, quick, hide somewhere
numb nuts, over there, over by the Mad Mouse. That's it,
squeeze in under there now, never mind the mud. Where is
he? Can't rightly tell with the noise of this rain.

Miii-key. I know you're here somewhere.

I ain't, I ain't here. You gots to convince him you ain't
here. He told you what would happen if you tried to run
again. Can't let him catch you.

Don't make this more difficult than it has to be. Come
out where I can see you.

You gots to be shittin' me. 'Bout six million ways to die
round here. I ain't comin' out, Ben. You'll just have to find me.

Come on, Mikey, it's just you and me. You know I'll
find you eventually.

An' I know what'll happen if you do, motherfucker. I is
wrecked. Fact it's just you out there in the rain, if that's even
true, means you got one thing in mind. No witnesses. Nobody
to see what really happened to Mikey Dempster. Damn,
probs nobody ever find me neither, less'n they fishes my body
from the river a week from now. Forget that promotion you
done promised me. You is surely takin' this opportunity to
remove this particular thorn from yo' ass, probs on Steph's
instructions. An' even if that ain't the truth, I know you

gots to be thinkin' 'bout it an' I am not takin' the risk. Pass on by, solja boy. Just leave me be an' I won't bother you no more, scout's honour.

Fucken sick of this, Mikey. If you come out now, I'll think about letting you off.

The fuck you will. I's gonna take one to the dome here, I just know it. Oh, he sounds close an' I ain't real well hid under here. He's gonna see me fo' sho'. Should I make a run for it? Fuuuck. Fuck it, I'm goin', head for the hills, son, go round the Mad Mouse an' double back to the carousel, maybe he already looked there an' I can fool him, s'got to be my only shot. S'not like I's gonna outrun the motherfucker so c'mon, work that crutch, that's it boy, pump it, use the rain as cover, you can make it, shit, lost my shoe in the mud, fucken leave it, leave it, don't stop movin' till you gets there. Only another couple metres an' that's it, you made it, you're there.

Stop. Take a breather. Wipe that mud off yo' bandages. That Nike slip-on's still out there but he ain't gonna see it, is he? Never mind that now, can't be worryin' 'bout it so just climb on up onto the carousel best you can, dawg, an' see if you can get under one of them covers, yeah, that's good, that's great, he ain't gonna spy you under there, no way.

Mikey.

Don't turn round. Don't turn round. He won't do nothin' if you don't turn round. A'ight, maybe just a look, just a glance so's I know fo' sho' it's him an' see if he's got any crew with him. I hope so, oh please don't let him be alone.

I see you.

Ben. Wait, brother, I can explain. I got separated from the others an' I got caught short an' when I come out the toilet you was all gone. I've just been wanderin' round here wonderin' what to do. Shit, I's glad to see you, really. Sorry I didn't come out before, I was just scared, you know? It's good you come back for me, I'd probs have died of hypothermia out here, dawg, knowhumsayin'?

I won't lie to you, Mikey. This is not good. I've had enough. I can find someone else—I don't need the hassle anymore.

It's like that, huh? Just toss me aside like I is nothin'? You bastard. A'ight, let me gather my thoughts here for a second, oh and by the way, go fuck yourself, homes. There, I said it. Fuck. You. You ain't never owned me, a'ight? My name is Michael Dempster and I have always been free, an' that's the triple truth, Ruth. I had twenty-one years of this shit. I'm cashin' in my chips, motherfucker.

That's why I'm here.

What you waitin' for then, dawg? Double tap, right here, 'tween the eyes. Don't leave me hangin'. What? What you lookin' for now?

You *hear* that?

What? What the fuck, you...damn, what *is* that?

I don't know. Sounds like...the ocean, kinda?

Oh. Oh shit. It ain't the ocean, dawg, but it might as well be. Wall of water 'bout six feet high comin' down the alley, swallowin' up everythin' in its path. A tsunami, headin' straight for us, an' we ain't got nowhere to run.

Can't run anyways. Hold on, hold on to that horse on a pole, wrap yo'self round there best you can an' brace for impact, homeboy, 'cos here it comes.

High ground. Gots me the one up on you at last, Corporal Wallace. Yeah, hang on there, motherfucker. You gots the guns for it, anyways. Link those big fucken Conan the Barbarian arms of yours round the steps. You is on the merry-go-round now, huh? Ain't so fucken funny anymore, is it, dawg? Keep on clutchin', water hittin' you in the face an' shit, that nice an' cool on your neck, bra? Oughta pop you in the mouth with my one good foot here, knock you into that dirty stream.

That be mad flow, dawg, all sorts of shit caught up in that wave, branches an' boxes an' cuddly toys an' some nasty lookin' sharps, better protect ya freak neck, brother. Seems like half the Kingdom gettin' washed away in the storm here, an' where the *fuck'd* all this water come from, s'like we is caught in a river or somethin'.

Pitiful. You is lookin' real pitiful over there, reachin' out all desperate like, hopin' I is gonna pull you aboard my ark. Ready to off me just a minute ago, an' now you wants my help. Lordy be. Don't you just love life's little ironies?

But hold up. Damn, them waters is creepin' higher. This be one epic flood, dawg. *Biblical.* An' maybe there's a door openin' for you here, Mikey. Maybe there's a way out. Is that a flashing EXIT sign I see, hangin' over your head, Ben-*jamin*? If I pull you on board the good ship Delta, we is quits, you feel me? Whatever done happened 'tween us is forgotten.

My slate be wiped clean, homes, and I walks right the fuck out of here today. Or swims. Whatevs. You down with that? Cross your heart an' hope to die?

A'ight. S'all good, yo. Grab my hand an' climb on up here, we'll ride these horsies through this wave like jet skis. Giddy-up.

Make haste, motherfucker. That be one big piece of metal just floated past. Think that was part of the fucken Ferris wheel right there. Kingdom be comin' down round our ears.

Come on, hoist yo'self up. I can't, I can't pull any harder, man. Barely grippin' on here myself. Ain't my fault I's not pumped like you. Had to cancel my gym membership when you done took a hammer to my ankle, dawg, 'member that?

Easy, hey, go easy, you's gonna pull me in, 'stead of the other way round. I'm tryin', you think I'm not tryin'? You 'bout twice my weight, solja boy. Come on, use them legs an' step up, less'n you wants to sleep with the fishes tonight.

Ben! Ben, hurry up, man, there's a car comin', a fucken car an' it's draggin' all sorts of big shit with it. You got to get out of there, man.

No. No, no, come on! Move! That's it, you's nearly there. One final heaaaave an'…

Oh shit.

He let go. He's gone.

It hit him. That car just rolled right up like a great white an' plucked him off the steps of the carousel. The look on his face. Oh man, I was lookin' right in his eyes as it crushed his legs an' his fingers opened an' he let go an' then he was gone. Sucked under the water, under all that metal an' there he is, way over there already, bobbin' back up, face down, nothin' but a ragdoll, all mashed up an' lifeless. Oh Christ, he's wrecked, he's done. It all happened so fast an' I couldn't do nothin', I swear.

Hold up, I's in trouble myself over here. I don't like the sound of that creakin' noise. This ride ain't supposed to be operational. Come on, horsey, don't you be turnin' round that way, that ain't good for me. Gonna get my hand stuck in there, better watch. Oh fuck, I've gotta, oh, I'm goin' in.

Take a breath, son. It's gonna be all right. Just dive into that flow an' start kickin'. It's the only way out.

Down an' down I spiral, way deeper than I even thought was possible. I keep my eyes open so's I can see what's happenin'. It ain't completely dark down here. The headlights of cars light the way as they tumbles on past me. I ain't scared for some reason. I's kinda calm, like I's floatin' inside the belly of some big fish that done swallowed up half the world. I look down below an' it ain't the dirt of sideshow alley like I 'spect but a big crack in the ground. Whole houses is fallin' into this pit, driftin' real slow down to the depths. Sun loungers an' bikes an' toasters an' kettles an' Xboxes with their leads trailin' behind move in a swirlin' orbit of the homes, fish feedin' on divin' whales.

There's people down here too. Don't notice them at first but if I squints through the gloom I can see one or two of 'em hangin' there. Shadowy divers clingin' to their porches, or sittin' behind the wheels of their Toyota Camrys, starin' out the windshield like they's waitin' for someone to explain what in hell's happenin'.

I'm floatin' through an underwater Queensland. Broken fences an' cats hissin' bubbles, rider-less motorcycles an' rusted ol' shipping containers, the Ferris wheel an' carousel, confused-lookin' seagulls an' kiddlywinks with wonder writ on their faces, all swirlin' down into the vortex, vanishin' into the gaping mouth of the earth. I can see Ben way over there, his T-shirt torn an' stained with blood, burns on his neck an' chest exposed, the side of his skull split open where that car musta clocked him in the dome. His waist is all crushed and broken, his legs turned at a weird angle like he's tryin' out some mad dance moves. Ring of crimson round him like a hula hoop. Must be the way the current's draggin' him but it sure looks like he's raisin' one hand to his bleedin' temple to salute.

I stop fallin' then an' just hover in place as best I can like some human starfish while the whole world rushes on by. I watch Ben as he gets sucked into the whirlpool, slowly turnin', his arms outstretched. Another couple seconds an' he's gone, vanished into the darkness. That's when I see the light up above an' strike out for it, swimmin' for all I's worth till I break the surface an' claw my way to land.

Don't know this place. Floodwater musta swept me right on out the showgrounds an' into another part of Toowoomba. Manage to crawl on out the water onto a muddy incline by grabbin' the roots of some big tree. Need to rest. I's beat. Ain't rainin' here an' my foot's throbbin' like a mofo. Glad I done cut that cast off. Might've been a different story otherwise. Might've ended up like Ben, down there somewhere with the crabs eatin' his eyes.

No time to think 'bout that. Gotta keep movin' 'fore I gets caught by the flood again.

Grab that branch there, Mikey. Yeah, that'll do nicely as a crutch. Get yo'self into those trees. Water. So much water. S'like the ocean done rose up to claim the land. Holy shit, all sorts of critters runnin' for cover in here an' they don't seem to be too concerned 'bout a human in their midst. Roos an' birds an' even snakes boltin' from the flood. Everything headed for high ground, though it didn't seem to matter none up here in Toowoomba.

Where am I, dawg? Trees all around, drippin' wet, the sun just peekin' through the clouds up there in the canopy, beams of light coursin' 'tween the branches that're crawlin' with bugs clamberin' over each other to get off the forest floor. Everythin' desperate to cling onto whatever life they gots an' I is too, staggerin' an' stumblin' through this strange place, lookin' for a way out an' sure of only one thing. Somehow, I'm alive. Praise be to Kanye.

Break in the trees up ahead. Looks like a road. No water. Couple of wallabies bounce out ahead, streak across the bitumen. Hear a horn in the distance. Somebody comin'. Keep goin', son. Work that crutch. You're almost there. This time, baby, this time.

Yo, hey, some help over here. Yeah, that's it, hit the brakes, dawg, you gots to watch out for those critters anyhow. Big roo'll come crashin' through your windscreen an' kick you upside the head. Homeboy's got hissel a bitchin' ute though, bullbar an' everythin'. Guess these Queenslanders is used to pile-drivin' their way through the wildlife.

Is he reversin'? Nah, s'all good, dawg, I'll come to you. Just hold up, it ain't easy with this old branch. Damn, I is a mess. Not exactly presentable for strangers, but these is hard times an' ain't nobody gonna refuse me a ride, even if I is bleedin' an' hobblin'.

Brother, am I glad to see you. Roll down that window an' let's get a look-see at yo' clock. Mekong Delta from upriver be back up on the stage, my flow restored now I's out of that cage, help a homeboy out at the very least, your ride is dope maybe yeti some might even say beast, yo all I's hearin' out here is the sounds of silence, y'all better open up or there's gonna be some violence, I be Mekong Delta an' I shouldn't haveta shout, this song is over, that's the end, *c'est fini* and I'm out, out, out.

O DARK HUNDRED

There's a certain time of the morning that not many people ever see. If you've hit the sack at a reasonable hour, like any normal person, chances are you'll be sleeping deeply, way down in some dream world where no one can touch you. If your house was on fire, you probably wouldn't know until it was too late. The only people who're awake at that time are usually up to no good.

At the height of summer in Uruzgan, you're talking four-thirty, four-forty in the morning. Technically, it's sunrise or dawn, but those words just didn't seem right in that context. They didn't belong there. 'Sunrise' made it sound like there might be a good day ahead, bringing with it the prospect of laughter and friendship, of a day at the beach with the family, or of some fucken chirpy chat-show host with a face plastered in make-up to cover the bags under their eyes giving you the minor-celebrity lowdown. In the service, you called it o dark hundred.

If you were awake then, you were either going to kill someone or get killed. No two ways about it. You would ghost out of the compound in Humvees or choppers, sometimes on foot, locked into the eerie green world of your night-vision goggles, PlayStation for real. It would be cold but you knew, you could almost sense the heat ready to slosh like a coat of fresh paint over the face of the mountains. You had to go in fast and hit whoever you were told to hit while they were stretching and yawning and wiping the sleep from their eyes.

The crackle of Ludowyk's voice in your ear. *Second squad, move up. Fan right. Watch your six.* Then someone else, a throaty whisper, maybe yours. *Five hostiles, Ludo. Permission to engage.*

Schwack 'em.

Ftt-ftt-ftt.

Bullets passing through the silenced barrel of an M4. Green laser streaks lighting up the night vision. The sound of someone crumpling in a heap, probably thinking they were still dreaming. A flurry of activity as whoever those strangers were, enemy or friend, combatant or civvy, guilty or innocent, realised that devils walked among them. The absolute focus of adrenaline surging through your veins, and maybe, if you and Ludo had time before leaving the operating post, something else in the bloodstream too. A microscopic crystal army, charging across the synapses, lending you an edge those others out there in the darkness did not have. You never feared death with glass in your heart. You were death. You devoured souls, to make up for the ones you'd left behind, somewhere along the way.

A grenade would go off, or a lightning bolt from the underside of a hovering Valkyrie, and the night scope would burn a wall of digital green into your eyeballs. You would flip the goggles down and let them dangle around your neck, blink to adjust to the shadows, and finish the job. Sometimes you would take pictures, just in case you'd stumbled upon one of the Big Bad Wolves.

And then you'd be gone, climbing into a truck or a Blackhawk, Ludo performing a head count, even if someone had lost their head. Wiping blood spatters from your gear, not knowing whose it was. You'd roll or fly on out of there, still buzzing, index finger aching to keep pulling. You'd know what time it was from the glow on the horizon. Sunrise. Dawn. O dark hundred. Soon, you'd be having breakfast. Eggs, maybe. Cereal. Coco Pops, for that glorious sugar hit.

You haven't felt that way in years, but you feel it now. It's dark, but there's a glow, a hum, a stillness. It's peaceful down here. The pain in your legs and in your head and on your neck is nothing but a distant throb, a reminder of something you've already forgotten. You just want to drift, to float. Close your eyes, Corporal. The mission's over. You're Oscar Mike.

Hold on. Just a second. Not yet.

You are standing at the back of the tent, watching your mum onstage. You're not supposed to be there. If Dad finds out, he'll punch you in the ear like he did last time. You don't see what the big deal is. Yeah, she's in the buff, but she's your mum. It's the tattoos and the sword you want to see anyway, not her titties. That's what everyone else, the leering goons who line up dozens deep, pay for.

She's a great dancer. Moves like a snake. And you love that ink on her back. A three-masted sailing ship being pulled under the waves by a kraken. Look at the detail. Seagulls gliding overhead, waiting to scavenge the spoils when the boat sinks, to pluck out eyeballs from floating corpses. Sailors tumbling from the rigging, some of them in the water already, their eyes wide and filled with terror. The tentacles of the beast curl up over her right shoulder as she dances, like it's climbing her body, trying to infiltrate the garden scene on her chest.

Roses. Hundreds of tiny roses in bloom covering her breasts, and below is a wrought-iron gate, open just a fraction to suggest there might be a way to climb right inside her belly, to discover her secrets, to see what's in there.

Yours is weak by comparison. A slobbering hound, the symbol of the Bluedog. It hurt like fuck. Made you feel soft. Gave you a newfound respect for your old mum, though. She could handle pain. She had to, putting up with Francis all those years. You wonder what they're doing now, right this minute. The old man's probably dozing in the chair, a half-drunk tinnie spilled on the rug next to his trailing arm. Evalisse will be watching some reality cooking show. *Master-chef. My Kitchen Rules.* She loves that shit. Has a thing for George Calombaris. Never understood her taste in men.

You suppose Steph will be the one who has to tell them. Better her than Huw. Too much bad blood between him and Francis.

Shit, now look where you are. The Channel Ten studio, stood behind a stove and a sink and a bunch of expensive chopping boards. You're wearing an orange jumpsuit and your ankles are chained together. There's a hard-looking con at the bench in front of you, and another glowering behind. It's year five of a forty stretch and you've picked up a few skills in the kitchen at Barwon. All you have to do is make it to the end of the season and you're home free—pardoned, the chance to write your own cookbook and maybe host a show on SBS. *Carny Food* with Benjamin Wallace, winner of *Cook for Your Life!*

Mikey's grinning from ear to fucken ear. He loves that you're on his show, that you can see how well he's done, that he was right all along. He's a star now, a genuine media phenomenon. You're in his shadow. It's embarrassing. But if that's what it takes to get out of there, you'll play along.

It gets worse. You're in the audience at the Grammys. He's just won album of the year. *The Kingdom of the Blind* has gone platinum. Fifty Cent hands him the trophy. They embrace like old friends. Mikey slaps him on the back and they share a private joke. The crowd is on its feet. They want to hear the new single, the duet with Pharrell. Miley Cyrus is weeping in the corner, a broken woman, her career in ruins. She is pregnant with Mikey's child. No one pays her much attention.

He thanks you in his speech.

If it weren't for my homeboy Corporal Wallace, I wouldn't be here today, and that's the triple truth, dawg. Peace out.

He raises two fingers in a victory salute. You don't know whether to laugh or cry.

Steph is waiting for you when you get out of prison and the publicity tour for the show is over. Being inside her is like pulling on the jeans you've owned for the better part of a decade. You know exactly where to go and how much wiggle room there will be. After all those years, sex between you isn't thrilling or romantic or weird anymore—it's intense catch-up fucking, throughout which you are bemused by the madness and strangeness of it all.

All that time you spent waiting for your life to begin. The years of expectation, of yearning for your real friends to arrive, the ones who would take your hand and lead you away to a better life, the one you were *supposed* to have, they just slipped away somehow. And now you're older, you're working in a restaurant, quietly serving up dishes to customers who remember you from that crazy cooking show where everyone died but you. They know you used to be a meth dealer, and a carny, and a soldier, and a boy who watched his mother swallow swords—but it's a past that is so dim and distant it feels like someone else's, or a tall tale you once heard whispered on sideshow alley.

Bad habits, casual opinions, your reluctance to engage with the world—it's a human fire sale at your place. Everything must go. You decide to spend whatever precious time you have left in this world bidding farewell to a man who, in truth, you never liked very much anyway. His departure will not be lamented.

You and Steph rent a little place on the Sunshine Coast, in Mooloolaba maybe. You have an old Holden in the garage that needs some work. A legion of bottle tops is scattered around the floor. Every time you have to untangle the Gordian knot of extension cords, you promise yourself that you will replace them with a single, brightly coloured ten-metre one from Kmart. You collect snow domes from op shops. You have ones from Denver, Helsinki, Aberdeen.

Steph tolerates your fondness for vintage *Playboy*. Your favourite centrefold is Michele, playmate of the month, April 1978. She looks down on you from above the workbench, keeping watch as you work on the engine of the Holden. You know her body about as well as you do Steph's. She wears knee-length white stockings. A silk robe is swept back behind her hips. She is holding a parasol. Her eyelashes are heavy with mascara and if you look closely, and you have, there is a hint of make-up on her abdomen just above the thick blonde bush.

Michele was born in 1957 and enjoys making love on the beach, but only if it's warm out. She likes to hear the rhythm of the waves breaking against the shore and claims roller rinks are the best places to meet guys. She purports to be a direct descendant of Sir Francis Bacon. You wonder if he too was a prude in high school and loved to have his breasts kissed.

You imagine standing on the beach, watching as Michele strides out into the morning surf. She is in her sixties now, but still looks strong. Her skin is weathered and tough. The tendons in her neck strain with the chill of the waves. Her hands come up to the sun and she is momentarily framed on the horizon before thrusting beneath the water, stroking her way out effortlessly into the cobalt sea. If she gets into difficulties, there is no one to save her but you, and you are hardly qualified. You never were much of a swimmer. You always preferred the mountains. Getting up above everything. Looking down. Taking the high ground.

You wonder if there are answers to your questions out there at the bottom of the ocean, or in that former playmate's life, between the creases of her mottled skin. You want to ask Michele how she raised her children, if she taught them to swim and deejay and abseil, if their father showed them how to roller skate. Did they ever see the photos? Did they roll their eyes and say, 'Nice umbrella, Mum'?

The buttons of your jeans come open easily, though as you hop from one foot to the other awkwardly pulling them over your ankles, you see Steph waiting impatiently for you in bed, shaking her head at your clumsy antics. Be right with you, baby.

The cold of the water sucks the air out of you. You hold what little breath you have left until you see pinpricks of light, a galaxy swirling within your eyelids. You drift down, deeper, away from the surface until you are among the stars. You call the playmate's name.

Wait for me, Michele. Wait.

Somewhere an asteroid strikes the planet and, in an instant, you are vaporised and your atoms are rocketed high into the mesosphere. The man you were is now nothing more than a Triceratops, or maybe an Iguanodon. Either way, it's sayonara, big guy. You are megafauna, cast in the air by the impact, dashed into countless microscopic pieces.

The air is thin up there. It is hard to breathe. Everything looks so tiny. The night has passed. The horizon is ablaze with colour and light. The clouds part as the chopper begins its descent to the base and, finally, you turn and feel the sun's warmth on your face.

SCOTTISH BORDERS COUNCIL
LIBRARY &
INFORMATION SERVICES

ACKNOWLEDGEMENTS

Props to my editor David Winter for the fully sick remixes, publicists Jane Novak and Stephanie Speight for the media big-ups, and Chong for his beast cover skillz. Shout out to the posse at Arts Victoria for the chedda.

To the crew who put up with me and inspired me while I worked on this: David Astle, Jordan Bass, Nihal Bhagwandas, James Bradley, Sophie Cunningham, Jenny Niven, Diego Patiño, Nick Earls, James Franco, Robert Skinner, Afsaneh Knight, Andy Murdoch, Kent MacCarter, Mischa Merz, John Hunter, Jess Ho, George and Bonita at Zoologie, Brad Dunn, Yu-Ann Chen, Jason Crombie, Ianthe Brautigan, Tony Birch, Nadia Saccardo, Robert F. Coleman, Mel Cranenburgh, Bethanie Blanchard, Angela Meyer, Lisa Dempster, Jemma Birrell, Martin Shaw, Michael Williams,

Simon Abrahams, Michael Cathcart, Sarah L'Estrange, Estelle Tang, and Zora Sanders: Peace.

To the Destiny's Child of literature: Josephine Rowe, Claire Bidwell Smith, and Toni Jordan, whose books *Tarcutta Wake*, *The Rules of Inheritance*, and *Nine Days* taught me how to be a better writer: Holla!

To my family: Ernie and Liz, Julie and Sammy, Aunt Margaret and cousin Alison, Alun and Jenny, Barney and Alayna, and Tom: Can you kick it? Yes, you can.

To Eirian, whose propensity to sing filthy gangster-rap lyrics while she works would make Mikey proud.

SUGGESTED LISTENING

Kendrick Lamar
good kid, m.A.A.d city

Frank Ocean
Channel ORANGE

Azealia Banks
1991
Broke with Expensive Taste

A$AP Rocky
LONG.LIVE.A$AP

N.A.S.A.
The Spirit of Apollo

RL Grime
High Beams

ALSO AVAILABLE FROM TEXT PUBLISHING
CHRIS FLYNN'S DEBUT NOVEL
A Tiger in Eden

Belfast hard man Billy Montgomery is on
the run from the Northern Ireland police.

Where better to hide out than
Thailand's backpacker trail?

'Poignant…a cracking first novel.' *mX*

'Unmissable.' *Courier Mail*

TEXTPUBLISHING.COM.AU